For my parents

Mascot Books
560 Herndon Parkway #120
Herndon, VA 20170
info@mascotbooks.com

PRBVG1114A

Library of Congress Control Number: 2014917113

ISBN-13: 978-1-62086-798-3

Printed in the United States

www.mascotbooks.com

THE CRAVE

Kevin Enners

DEAR READER

The Crave takes place in the Boston area and spans many years. Over the years, crime, unemployment and overall economic health may have changed. To give this story continuity and consistency throughout, actual changes in these areas are not reflected. Please do not interpret this as a negative reflection of the Boston area. I can assure you this story is very enticing and has a plot that I hope you will enjoy thoroughly. Happy reading!

It's a strange world we live in. We live life nestled in our own safe beds, keeping to ourselves because we are too afraid to step into the real world and open our eyes to watch crime run rampant through our cities. Instead, we keep off the streets while gangs burn our cities to ash.

The streets of South Boston seemed so tough and rugged when I was a kid, but after some years living in the hellish dumps of the city, I had adapted to the gritty neighborhood I called my home. At night, I lay in my single bed wide awake, I could hear the helpless, mournful cries of a homeless man being beaten to death. The sorrowful thought that that man probably never stood a chance against those careless goons; and, the idea that it could have been one of my family members, haunted me in my sleep. I would lie in my cot, humming the lyrics to Bob Dylan's legendary solo, "House of the Rising Sun," drowning the agony that escaped the dying man's lungs, with Dylan's masterful guitar-strumming.

But, the hymn of the departed sang solos, resonating graphic nightmares of my family. Rivers of blood flowed underneath me as I perched on a seat of black sky, a panoramic view of the alley, witnessing gory atrocities. As the crimson tide rolled away, the sea of red left buildings and dumpsters crusted with gore. The putrid stench of warm blood wafted into the air, drilling my nostrils.

I would hover in mid-air in a coma as my family members were dragged from our home one-by-one by the neighborhood gang. Gang members cheered, circling my family like lions. The stand-off turned into a blood-bath as my father confronted the street thugs, defending my sister and mother as a courageous lion king protecting his pride from cackling hyenas. But despite his noblest of efforts, the king fell to his demise as the hyenas shredded my father to bits. My lungs and throat burned as I tried to ward off the belligerent goons. They leaped over my father as red gore leaked from every orifice on his face, circling Laurie and my mom, feasting off the timidity of lambs.

I bolted upright, coated in a film of sweat, away from the sticky, damp bed sheets that clung to me like a spider's web, awaking to the sickening blows of an excruciatingly painful death. Grisly, wet smacks of somebody's skull being bashed against a hard surface from the mugging boomeranged off the brick forest, lashing through the thin bedroom window, inducing restless nights and painting graphic murals upon the delicate canvas of my childhood memory – not that I'm complaining. I'm actually thankful for it.

Criminals treat everyone equally – like shit. I was born with cerebral palsy and, even though it only affects me on my left side, most of my friends and family treated me differently. As a kid, I use to be coddled by my parents more than most kids. It almost felt good to pretend to be a stupid kid being scolded by my surly neighbors. They taught me how to stand up for myself, my family, and my friends. I learned to shoot comebacks. I would banter back and forth with local drug-dealers, get a chuckle from them, and continue on my way. But then, I took it to another level.

Once, when I was twelve, I made the brash decision of rescuing an unfortunate soul, I climbed from my bed and strode toward my window and opened it. I stuck my head out and, filling my lungs with the night's tepid air, I screamed, "Cops!" and watched as the muggers fled from the alley. Dogs barked and lights sparkled in windows of neighboring houses as the occupants inside spotted the gang.

The police were much feared in South Boston in the mid-seventies, because that was when crime rates in the area were booming. The police eventually realized that South Boston was a breeding ground for the wicked and began taking serious measures to enforce the law. Unfortunately, this gave some cops the incentive to abuse their authority and they would become dirty.

Corruption in South Boston was contagious like an epidemic virus infecting every organism that entered. I'd see cops patrolling the streets of my neighborhood on my way to and from school. Occasionally, corrupt cops would pop by the neighborhood to bust some drug dealer during a "raid."

Our neighborhood was a hotspot for heroin and cocaine dealers. The neighborhood was littered with the vile drugs, which spurred more crime and violence. Whenever the neighbors cooked a fresh batch, hordes of customers would gather like zombies to get their fix. That also enticed dirty "pigs"; the customers who carried a shield for a cover, using it as leverage for free samples, and ultimately ruled my neighborhood of South Boston– known as Southie.

Routinely, when I came home from school, I'd see at least one police car parked outside of one of the run-down houses, with a smashed-in front door. Profanities polluted the musty air as a repertoire of blows from a nightstick slammed down on a drug dealer's head. I could not understand the police officer's business there. It was only when one cop stooped over the criminal, grabbed the powder, and snorted the narcotic from his palm, that I realized he wasn't there to serve justice.

"The fuck you looking at?" the cop growled. I, Mike Craven, the all-around smart-ass, stood there stone cold, at a loss for words. The cop's glaring eyes focused on my left arm, then on my face, his bloodshot stare was menacing, appallingly vicious.

"Hey!" he barked. "I said what the fuck you looking at, cripple?" He wielded his nightstick as fear ran down my spine. The graphite-colored club was matted with smears of blood that dripped from the tip. I looked into the cop's dilated pupils teeming with anger. The cop shoved his gun in my face. My eyes grew wide as I stared into the barrel of a Glock 9mm; unarmed, I was playing Russian roulette with a fiend.

"Michael Patrick Craven, inside. Now!" Mike's mom yelled. He submissively backed away, indecisive of whether he was bold enough to turn his back on the crooked cop. Heroin-addicted police officers were among the many devils scouring the streets. For the most part, Mike lived secluded in his home, away from the malicious drug-dealers that his father had warned him about. His father, Patrick Craven, was an undercover detective, working for the Boston police. He worked as an inside man on gang-related crimes, observing and reporting heinous felonies. His primary target – the Irish mob.

Illegal substances were readily dispensed by an underground railroad of drug lords. South Boston was a terminal organism in the metropolis; slowly deteriorating by the day and steadily growing ill from harboring corruption.

Every South Boston household lived in fear of the Irish mob, who casted a large, watchful shadow over the entire city of Boston. Rumors dispersed that a local neighborhood gang, the Q-block, was a cabbage-patch, where the Irish mob-boss could handpick the next generation of mobsters. Proud of this, Q-block gang members would parade through Southie's streets and embrace rivalry, competing for the most unscrupulous reputation, often throwing total lockdown on the town.

Tales of the notorious Q-block gang spread through Southie's network of schools. These tales of menace helped foster their tough reputation. They marked their territory by tying sneakers together and throwing them around telephone lines which towered over Mike as he walked home. Outsiders, not understanding the significance of the sneakers, wandered into gang territory. Mike would try and steer them away before the strangers were accosted by Q-block members. Those unfortunate to not heed his urging were quickly surrounded and overpowered by the gang.

One day, Mike saw the delinquents harass students between classes by shoving them into the metal lockers, pilfering their lunch money, taunting them, feeding off of their fearfulness. He studied their physiques, their strengths, and their weaknesses. They were big for middle school students. Mike estimated each one to be as tall as six foot, approximately one-hundred-and-eighty pounds, surely fully developed.

After being dismissed from class, Mike walked home. He thought about lunch; sitting next to his friend Kurt, from Dorchester, who boasted about his brand new watch. Its polished crimson face sparkled in the light as its white hands pointed to the noon hour. Mike feigned a smile. He didn't really care about the watch, but as Mike looked up, he saw the hoodlums staring at it like famished lions spying on their next meal, desire twinkling in their eyes.

Mike thought about this as he walked home around the periphery of gang territory in the late afternoon. As he traveled further down the road, screams wailed from a dark corner behind a liquor store. The familiarity of the boy's screams caused nausea, as Mike hoped the unlucky prey was not whom he thought. Mike raced towards the ghetto-grown clique; the ripe stench of weed drilled his nose. Mike watched massive knuckles being wielded in the air, like a sledge-hammer, pulverizing his friend. Kurt moaned in excruciating pain and dropped to the ground where he remained curled in a ball as he absorbed the Southies' annihilating kicks to his face and body.

Those assholes were at least twice the size of Kurt. What to do? Mike couldn't risk abandoning Kurt to flag down help, potentially leaving him for dead. As his father's mantra, "never start a fight, but if ya have to, always finish one," resonated in his mind, Mike mustered the courage to bail his friend out of the lion's den.

"Hey!" Mike screamed. "The fuck you doing?!" his distinct South Boston accent coated his words. His heart pulsated with nervous excitement as he dashed into gang territory. Mike passed the shoes hanging from the telephone lines, as an eerie feeling of being alone in uncharted waters washed over him. He fought his nervousness and plunged into the circle of sharks. One of the sharks stepped away from Kurt and flipped open a pocket-knife, attempting a worthless try at intimidating Mike. The young man had a rugged chiseled face cropped with red facial hair. The brawny thug shot back, "The fuck you care?!"

Mike remained unwavering and, feeling a concentrated dose of adrenaline shoot through his weak left side, pitched a cannon that careened into the thug's chin. As Mike threw the roundhouse hook, he saw the thug writhe back, teetering on his heels. The punch was not quite enough to paralyze him but definitely enough to momentarily stifle him. The pack turned their attention to Mike as the dazed thug massaged his chin. Sneering, two members pounced on Mike from the left side and tackled him, wrestling him to the ground. Most of Mike's strength came from the right side of his body; he could write, grasp, or pull just about anything with his right hand. But, Mike's left side was much weaker because his muscles were atrophied from the cerebral palsy.

Feeling confident they had neutralized "the cripple", the thugs released the half-Nelson hold turning their attention back to Kurt. Mike sprang up, astonishing his attackers. Despite his seemingly useless arm, he was too swift for them, too cunning. Appearances can be deceptive, Mike wanted to yell. Tapping into his inner fighter, Mike balanced out his lack of brawn with cunning techniques. He knew how to hit twice as hard with more accuracy than as his opponent. Mike had wrangled street brutes before. The level of confidence they had in themselves had worked against them. They were clumsy and slow, relying on intimidation and reputation to win fights. A constant stream of adrenaline coursed through Mike as odorous smells wafted from the crowd, inducing a wave of dizziness over him.

Suddenly, Mike felt a numbing sensation crawl through his fingers, ascending through his bicep, locking his right shoulder as one of the goons wrenched his arm back. Mike leaned back on the goon and rammed his left elbow into his attacker's ribs. Mike could feel the branches of bone cracking as both landed onto the decaying asphalt. Lying awkwardly on a pillow of hoodlums that cushioned his fall, Mike frantically scrambled over the gang members towards Kurt. Kurt collected himself, blood running down his face, and rose to his feet looking at Mike, dazed.

"Run, Kurt!" Mike hollered at his confused friend, tugging him along with a fistful of t-shirt. Kurt's eyes flickered, as if realizing the seriousness of the situation for the first time. Breaking away from Mike's grip, he sped off, dashing at full speed, trailblazing his escape route like a Thoroughbred sprinting through the Kentucky Derby's last quarter mile, leaving Mike in his wake.

As he vaulted over the bullies who clawed at his ankles like the undead, a blade of panic cut into Mike's back as he sensed the hounds ditching their quarry for a much more vulnerable target, "the cripple." It was not long before Mike heard loud footsteps rambling after him, their rhythm pulsating in his eardrums like *The Tell-Tale Heart*. The Q-block harassers were hot on Mike's trail.

Another dose of dwindling adrenaline shot through Mike's blood-heated veins like a rushing river at the end of its course. Stinted blades of hair cropped up on his neck. The unforgiving pavement punched the soles of his tennis shoes, rattling his joints. Mike gasped the muggy September air, as late afternoon turned to dusk. *I have to lose them*, Mike thought. He knew of a secret path he could disappear through, camouflaged by a maze of multi-family homes. He had to get back home to Dorchester, where Ma was probably making supper. He wound through the opaque brush of the shadow-cast alleyways, sprinting as fast as his legs could carry him, but he could still hear the Southies huffing and puffing behind him.

Sweat poured down his burning face, dripped into his eyes and seeped between his thirsty lips. He peered over the peak of his bony shoulder to gauge the distance between himself and his pursuers. Their pasty faces were drenched with fatigue. At last, the chase cooled; forfeited by the South Boston gang. Out of the corner of Mike's eye, he saw them shaking their heads in disbelief and frustration. Their grumbles echoed for blocks.

"Fuck!" he heard one of the Southies wheeze. The echo dispersed throughout the deadpan traffic as a tide of red, pink, and yellow hues spread across Boston. Very few ventured into this neck of Boston.

Mike downgraded his pace to a curt stroll, observing the colorful brushstrokes of pink and orange painted by the setting sun. As he flicked sweat from his head, he estimated by the setting sun that the hour was between five and six o'clock. He refused to wear a watch because, at least to him, it was symbolic of "poindexters", the mathematical wizards who develop love affairs with nonsense numerical equations they enjoyed creating to torture less-gifted minds. However, he knew any delays on the journey home were deemed inexcusable by Craven's Supreme Court judges, his parents. Mom, he knew, would be mad that he was late for supper.

"Shit!" he muttered to himself. Mike arrived at the two-story tenement, where he noticed his fourteen-year-old sister, Laurie, perched atop the steps, balancing a textbook on her knees as she scribbled in deep thought. A pair of headphones wrapped around her head with a wire connecting the earpiece to a portable cassette player that was clipped to the waist-band of her jeans. Mike watched the gears grind in her mind as Laurie, apparently baffled, tried to decode her homework.

Outside doing homework, bad sign thought Mike. Laurie was like a sparrow sheltering from a storm. Mike knew his parents were, yet again, in another volatile fight. As Laurie completed homework assignments, nestled under the flickering porch light, the night air offered a serene resort in which thoughts were undisturbed. Mike knew this. He also knew by the muffled, gruff voices that echoed from within that his parents were in the middle of a wicked argument. *Had to be about work again*, thought Mike.

The rumble of an engine droned through the solemn street interrupting Mike's contemplations; he sensed danger lurking around the corner. Goosebumps cropped up on the back of his neck as a slow chill of threat blew by. Mike sharply turned to locate the potential threat. A 1971 forest green Chrysler Fury slowly crept by his house. He gazed into the vehicle's window as it rolled down. A sneer appeared on the face of the goonish driver. Mike recognized the South Boston thug he had encountered moments before. The thug's eyes darted from Mike and narrowed on Laurie. The thug flirted with Laurie. Mike gritted his teeth and stepped in front of Laurie, shielding her from the stalkers. The thug sneered at Mike once more, before the car was thrust into gear, and peeled away. *That's right*, Mike thought, *run away*.

"Who was that?" Laurie asked, concerned.

"No one," he replied, turning back to the stoop, shooing away her worries. He knew better than to blabber about his encounters with the Q-block gang. In that instant, Mike was conscious of his throbbing legs that urged him to sit down. He plunked heavily down upon the crusty stoop and tapped his hand over the center of the textbook, diverting Laurie's inquisitiveness. She did not need to worry about the senseless scraps that he bailed his friends out of, they were not her concern. "Curiosity killed the cat," he replied, turning his back to her.

"Whatever," Laurie mumbled. "Ass," she muttered and looked up at him. *Gets her every time*, Mike chuckled.

The heat of Laurie's agitation emitted from her palm as she landed a harsh smack on his shoulder. "Ouch! Okay, okay. Stop," Mike chuckled as he begged for a cease-fire. "How are you?" He asked, ignoring his throbbing shoulder. "I'm surviving," Laurie grimaced. Laurie nodded toward the yelling back in the abode. Mike turned and faced the front door. He knew if he were to be so brazen to burst through the front door, he would be an unwanted intruder. His parents were not prone to fighting except for the occasional dispute all couples endured in marriage. This, however, signaled something big was brewing. Suddenly, Mike watched as his father burst out the front door, frazzled and brooding, fumbling with car keys.

"Hi, Dad." Mike grasped at his father's attention, as he bolted to his feet, trying to make his presence more ostensible and, also, to distract Patrick Craven from whatever infuriated him.

"Hi, pal," Paddy Craven shot back automatically, deflecting Mike's plea for attention. "Here," Paddy mumbled as he tossed his Boston PD badge to Mike. Mike stared at his dad confused. "Keep it safe 'till I come back," Paddy said as he winked at Mike.

Mike sensed a bleak cloud looming over his father. Paddy seemed to be in distress. His frown reflected in the window of his car. Mike noticed a flicker of something he had never seen in his father's stridently fearless eyes. That shadow lurking in the corner of Paddy's eye was fear, true fear. Mike knew that fear and it overwhelmed him. A sense of panic was churning inside Paddy which quickly spread to Mike like a contagious disease.

Paddy's Ford Taurus sped away into the night, abandoning Mike who felt ill with unease. A sharp kick-in-the-gut, Mike knew something was about to go down. A storm was sure to come, but no one could have ever prepared for the destruction that was to follow.

Mike felt Laurie tugging on his pant leg. "Hey, I'm down here," Laurie said. "Sorry," Mike shrugged, shrouding his concern. His thighs seared with flames of soreness. Mike could not grasp the strong commitment his father had to the undercover life of a Boston police detective. Why did he perpetuate his role as an infiltrator of the Irish mob, to put his life in never-ending danger for the Boston PD. The only reason was that Paddy needed to not only establish, but to sustain, a strong bond with the head-honcho, Jack Flanagan, aka Flintlock.

Mike pondered this as he rested on the stoop, massaging his burning thighs. A sickening feeling boiled his stomach, and Mike didn't know if it was from sprinting for half a mile or his father's abnormally aggressive behavior.

Laurie shrugged and shook her head. "Ya want to help me with Algebra?" she asked. He smiled and answered, "Laurie, you're two grades above me." "So?" she responded. Mike laughed and explained, "So, ya probably know about that stuff more than I do."

"Maybe, maybe not," she retorted. Mike sighed, knowing that he couldn't win this battle. It was nighttime, but the sky still framed powerful rays of light, and the neighborhood was sleeplessly mulling around. Clans liked to barge out of the darkness from their dungeon-like homes to breathe in the night's late-summer air before returning to their stuffy quarters to begin the next batch of narcotics. Feeling tired from rescuing Kurt from those goons earlier, Mike wanted an excuse for just marching inside and vegetating instead of helping Laurie with her homework. The light mounted beside the door emitted bright light that shone down on Laurie's inquisitive face. "Alright," Mike groaned.

"The old ways are the best," Flanagan mused, sitting in his black Lincoln, snuffing out a would-be traitor. Jack 'Flintlock' Flanagan liked his nickname, 'Flintlock', because to him, the Flintlock rifle superseded modern firearms, just as he superseded most organized crime. He stared at the pages of the report of mob activities, conscripted by the various criminal entities embedded in his organization. It discussed the Upper Echelon Program, an FBI informant network, which bargained for criminals to have complete immunity from arrests if they provided law enforcement with sound intelligence on criminal activities that resulted in arrests. The FBI used the Upper Echelon Program when all sources for information came up empty. It was their last resort. This contract brewed controversy among local law enforcement agencies and mob families nationwide.

Local police departments were kept in the dark. They were never told who the mob informants were nor had access to the information provided by the informants. The FBI worked as an insulated entity. Taking the issue further, many police departments argued that cooperation with criminals gave crime networks opportunity to mislead them while informants got away with more crimes. The Boston Police continued with their own ways of infiltrating the mob and gaining evidence. Mob families, already paranoid of any deviation within their ranks, became even more suspicious of each other. A slight change from "normal behavior" was evidence enough for a member to be taken out.

The Upper Echelon Program created an uneasy environment.

Flanagan had been burned too many times by a trusted wingman that turned "confidential informant" because of this program, just to save his own ass. This was almost as insidious as law enforcement infiltrating the mob, a dangerous proposition for the infiltrator. Faced with bookend threats, Flanagan was continuously wary of all his contacts. Paddy Craven was his latest concern. Just recently, he had Paddy Craven's landline tapped, which produced confirmation of a leak. Now, Flanagan's old-fashion surveillance commenced as he observed his confidant, Patrick Craven, in a phone booth whispering. Flanagan's neck hairs perked up like antennae.

"Yeah, I'll see you then. Corner of Commonwealth? Sure." Craven hung up and looked around sheepishly as Flanagan melted into the shadows.

Flanagan tailed Craven to Commonwealth Avenue. He remained four cars behind the Ford Taurus, camouflaged in a constellation of mid-size sedans.

Recently, Flanagan caught wind of a plot designed to terminate the highly contested Upper Echelon Program. The program was the only barrier keeping him from being incarcerated. Flanagan shuddered as he considered the implications he would face if his sanctuary burned to ashes. All of the people he "gave up" to the FBI would seek scathing revenge. Flanagan needed to act quickly and deliberately, he assured himself as he spied through his windshield, watching his ostensible friend wade through the crowd of pedestrians, putting on a marvelous act. He applauded Patrick Craven for his authentic performance as a mobster.

Craven stood on the street corner with his hands shoved in his coat pockets and wearing a pair of Aviator sunglasses, pretending to mingle with the crowd. He casually paced back and forth on the sidewalk as a man in a brown leather coat walked by. They crashed into each other as a crowd brushed past them, providing ideal cover.

They held their hands out apologetically, and kept going. *How coincidental*, Flanagan mused as he scratched his bottom lip. He felt a stroke of satisfaction, catching the infiltrator in the act. Craven disappeared around the corner at the end of Commonwealth. Now was the time for an intervention. Flanagan did not want the FBI involved. This was his business and the last thing he needed was the FBI sticking their grubby fingers in it. His bottom lip quivered as he tasted his anger and disgust. He opened his glove box and took out his loaded Beretta 92FS.

The plan went awry and Patrick Craven knew it. Paddy had given the last bit of intelligence to the agent when he fell under the collapsing railroad of deception. The bust hinged on the precipice of nailing the Irish mob boss Flanagan. Eyes beamed down Craven's neck. He knew then his cover was blown as he tugged the brim of the navy blue cap low over his eyes. He sensed the shadow in the dark sedan watching his every step. Paddy struggled to fight off the urge to make a run for it. He still needed to play the role as a normal pedestrian stretching his legs on an after-work stroll around Boston. Or, at least, that was his Captain's orders.

He felt his pistol under the leather trim of his coat, his police badge on his hip and heat blowing down his back. Paddy ducked behind his Taurus to the driver's side and looked around. He used the car as a shield while he spied, trying to pick up a visual on his watcher. He saw a dark Lincoln parked four cars behind his sedan with a dark figure that he did not recognize. As Craven paused, staring at the dark figure in the sedan, the heat that burned his neck quickly dissipated and an eerie chill gusted down his collar. Not wanting to waste any more precious time, Paddy decided to split. He revved the engine and sped away when three rounds pierced the trunk.

"Shit!" Paddy choked as he hit the gas. The automatic transmission groaned as the Taurus fishtailed onto Brookline Avenue. It gained speed as Paddy pressed a lead foot on the gas. He weaved between threads of cars, his heart pounding out of his chest. Paddy cut into the fast lane of I-93, gripping the steering wheel with panicked palms. Looking back through his rearview, headlights beamed at him, gaining on his bumper. He leaned on the gas, tearing between bumpers of flanking automobiles. Craven could feel the conducted heat of metal scarring metal as he squeezed between the throng of highway traffic.

Horns blared as Paddy sliced through four lanes. He glanced back as the Lincoln became gridlocked in a state of limbo. There was no escape for his tail, caught in a barrage of accelerating taillights. Paddy coasted down the exit ramp and heaved a sigh of relief. He loosened his clenched grip around the steering wheel's smooth, black coat of polyurethane as his vibrating nerves calmed. As Paddy drove through Southie, he flicked on a smooth jazz radio station to help lull his antsy mind. His cover was blown, he knew. Now was the time to get the hell out of Dodge.

There was no good shot. "Damn," Flanagan sneered, idly stroking the Beretta's trigger. He decided to hang back, out of Craven's sight. He did not want to waste bullets. He needed to adapt. Craven now became the Irish mob's number one threat. Flanagan's suspicion began when Beatty, his own crooked cop, gave him Craven's credentials from the local precinct. Flanagan didn't want to believe it. He liked Craven. Craven earned Flanagan's trust and loyalty, but this had cost him. Craven would pay with his life.

The sound of someone bursting through the front door jostled Mike from a series of dreams clouding his mind. Loud footsteps, a man's footsteps, trumpeted up from downstairs as an elephant tramples jungle floor. Laurie burst into Mike's bedroom, quickly locked the door behind her and climbed in bed with him yanking the covers over her head. Fear began to well in Mike's throat. He felt an eerie beat of vulnerability. "What's going on? "He quietly asked Laurie.

"Ssh!" Laurie put her index finger over her lips. "Dad's boss is here." Mike's fear turned to terror. His heart rocketed into his throat. Legends surrounding Flanagan detailed the rabid threat prowling inside his home. Mike hugged his sister for dear life, attempting to shroud the scent of pending death wafting through the ground floor rooms. As he tightened his grip around Laurie, he felt his sister's uncontrolled quivering.

"What were you doing meeting with that guy? Trying to bring me in, huh? You weasel."

"Flint-"

"Don't." Flanagan shouted in a nasally Boston accent, "I know you were trying to convince the bureau and the department to ditch the Echelon Program. You were ready to book me. I saw you bump into that guy."

"No. It was an accident."

"Bullshit! I watched you slip this into his pocket!" A beat of silence underlined deceit. Mike swore he heard Flanagan's voice crack. Although, he found it difficult to imagine ruthless Flanagan could feel anything.

The mob boss continued to rebuke Patrick Craven. Noise from a violent blow resonated through the house. Mike, visualizing the butt of a pistol bashing Patrick's head, cringed as a low ringing burned his ears. His blood boiled, listening to Flanagan's sadistic scolding. Mike's biceps burned as he reeled a crying Laurie closer to his chest. He tried to brace himself: not knowing what the erratic Flanagan's next actions were.

"I liked you, Paddy. I liked you a lot. But you leave me no choice. I'm about to burn your life and everything in it!" The gangster sounded livid.

"Please, don't bring my kids into this, Mr. Flanagan. Punish me, not them. They're too young… "

Mike cringed at sound of moans from Paddy as he groveled. Tears streamed down Mike's face as Paddy begged for the tortuous beating to end. A heart-wrenching moan Mike had never heard Paddy utter left a putrid taste on his tongue.

The boy's mom, Carlene, screeched furiously for mercy. "Shut up!" Another low Boston accent snapped as the hammer of a pistol clicked. Mike held his breath, stunned that his mother was being held at gunpoint. Then, somebody was slammed against a wall with a surprised grunt. Mike closed his eyes as the thunder inside the home clamored through the thin walls. He imagined his father pinning Flanagan against the thick slab of the house. He silently cheered Paddy on, clinging onto the slim chance of his parents retaliating and chasing the mob away. Unfortunately, his reverie quickly dissolved when he heard the plea continue through a howling chorus of nails scratching the linoleum floor, like the loser of a dog-fight being taken in for the kill. Then a deafening shot rang out. A loud thud on the downstairs floor beckoned to the cold, hard fact that his father was dead. Killed heartlessly in his own home. The devastating loss brought tears to his eyes and rage burned his face, branding Mike with a permanent lust for retribution.

"No, no..."

Mike heard Carlene beg, just as his father had. All it took was one bullet to shut her up forever. Time froze. Mike felt everything becoming sluggish. He felt beads of sweat raining from his brow, feeling his world disintegrate around him. Mike clasped his hands over Laurie's ears, hoping to spare her from the cries of despair. Laurie buried her tear-stained face into Mike's chest, as tears drained from his own eyes, as he cursed Jack Flanagan.

Heavy footsteps shook the dark world surrounding them, as the monster scaled the staircase. For every step Flanagan took, the boy's heart palpitated twenty beats faster, veins twitched in his neck as a concentrated river of blood was pumped by a rapidly beating heart. Flanagan's heavy footsteps echoed throughout the bungalow. Mike knew the time to fight was upon them. Mike primed himself to pounce as he rose to his feet, standing on the edge of the bed. Adrenaline and madness coursed through him as perspiration dripped from his face.

Laurie clawed at Mike's legs. "Wait." She tried to deter him from a brash action.

But, he ignored her, remaining staunch, ready to fight. His hands stiffened into claws. Teeming with hatred, Mike silently counted the beats winding down to the match. Five, four, three… His hands trembled as he balled them into firm clenched fists. Two, one…

The locked door was bashed in, projecting wooden bullets across the room that ricocheted off the adjacent wall. Though the bedroom was dimly lit, Mike could still see the blood that stained Flanagan's Armani suit and smell the stench that went with it. He wished he could hug his parents again. He wanted to taste his mother's cooking and play backyard football with his father and tell them that he loved them one last time.

Mike's first attack was deflected as Flanagan swatted him away with a vicious smack. Mike stumbled backwards, slamming into the wall. Mike's sinking heart rocketed into his throat and adrenaline surged through his body as he felt Laurie being snatched away. He lunged for Laurie with extended hands, but Flanagan stripped Laurie from Mike's grip. Laurie kicked and screamed as she was dragged into the devil's arms. Mike only saw red as he dove into the ring of fire, his heart smoldering. Death swarmed the room in suits as Mike clawed at Flanagan's neck.

Mike leaped onto Flanagan's back, trying to free Laurie from the clutches of the Irish mob boss. Flanagan's pin-striped Armani coat wrinkled as Mike wrapped his legs tightly around Flanagan's waist. Mike suddenly felt the claws of the boss' henchmen as they pried him from Flanagan's back when he shouted for them. But Mike fought back by wrestling Flanagan in a one armed chokehold, so desperately wanting to strangle him. Flanagan's Adam's apple bobbed against the crux of Mike's elbow, as the mobster gasped for breath and clawed desperately at Mike's arm.

Mike watched Flanagan's face turn rose red until the posse of demons clawed at his back. Revenge drew close as Mike slowly crushed Flanagan's throat. Muscle ligaments flexed throughout his arms as Mike watched Flanagan's face turn purple. Overpowered by the brute strength of the burly mobsters, Mike was torn away from Flanagan and tossed against the nearby wall, to which he was roughly pinned by Flanagan's posse. The numbing helplessness panged his nerves, while his back and head filled with throbbing pain.

The mobster that pinned him against the wall drew a pistol and aimed the barrel inches away from Mike's right eye as Laurie tried to escape the room by kicking Flanagan in the balls. She had barely dashed into the hallway when Flanagan hauled her back, tossing her on the bed. Mike's heart rocketed into his throat as he saw Flanagan extract his pistol from his belt and aimed it at Laurie's head. At that very moment, Mike's short life flashed before his eyes. Judging by Laurie's solemn look of defeat, she too knew that she was about to meet her maker. Mike and his sister were chained in line for death row. As he felt grim death reap his sister's soul, tears began to roll down Laurie's cheek. Mike's blood curdled as he was forced to witness Laurie's life end where the barrel of Jack Flanagan's Beretta began.

"No, stop. Please…" *This is it*, he told himself. A burn of feebleness defused through his neck and face. The emptiness of helplessness turned his anger into sadness. The fragrance of Flanagan's cologne suffocated him, wafting into his mouth and nose, winding up a coiled spring of bile which clogged Mike's esophagus, stifling his whimpering. Flanagan thumbed the hammer back, putting the wide-eyed Mike Craven under a loud spell of silence. Mike gulped down the fireball of fury smoldering in his esophagus.

"Say bye-bye, sweetheart. " Jack Flanagan said with a crooked grin painted on his whisker-shadowed face. Cued by Flanagan's demand, time coasted to a crawl. Sucked into the time-warp, Mike watched as Laurie's blood sprayed the walls in slow-motion.

The sound of police sirens blared throughout the streets. Flanagan and his men froze. While the ear-bursting cry diverted their attention, Mike slipped through the stalwart clutches of his captor as the grip of death loosened around his arm. Extended fingers jutted out from his crinkled palm, stabbing the mobster's eyes. The blinded suit tumbled backwards as he placed a beefy hand over his face.

"Shit!" The blinded mobster kvetched.

"Spread out!" Flanagan ordered. As the police charged through the front door, the clique members spread in different directions as they fled the crime scene in chaotic fashion, escaping with their lives. Mike sprang to his feet as the mafia members blazed their own escape route. Breaking glass resonated throughout the house as Mike sprinted toward the fleeing Flanagan, his bare feet pounding the frigid, hard wood floors. The two galloped down the steps as the BPD smashed the front door down.

Flanagan tore away from Mike's pursuit as they careened through the hall-way which was cornered off by a bonus room that overlooked the flashing blue lights surrounding the Craven residence. Burning with desire for revenge, Mike lengthened his stride and stretched his gait as far as he could to detain the man he wanted so badly to be imprisoned. Nipping at Flanagan's heels, Mike savagely closed the gap to practically arm's length. The wind current from the hallway air-conditioner blew the tail of Flanagan's Armani coat inches away from Mike. *If I could just...* Mike lunged for the coat tail. Flanagan crashed through the back window letting in crisp, cool night air. Shards of glass rained from the window as the mob boss fell, then raced away.

Mike sighed, filled with shame and guilt. He violently smacked the floor and collapsed into a sitting position, sulking over the mass destruction of his life. Mike clutched his knees to his chest. "Fuck!" he muttered, burying his face into his bare knees and weeping, ashamed he let the murdering sociopath blow his family to smithereens. The anger saturated his bones, cementing ir-reparable damage, making him feel hollow. Under his dreary cloud of distress, Mike admonished himself. *You could have stopped him*, guilt beckoned. *Why didn't you stop him?* He racked his brain for answers. *You could have stopped him.* His own pitiful wales bounced off the walls, reverberating back to him. *I should have had him. I should have sent him to hell!*

Throngs of police outside scattered in pursuit of Flanagan. Inside the floors squeaked as a pair of Oxfords subtly shuffled to Mike. A soothing aura engulfed Mike, massaging away his burrowing fury. He raised his head to meet a soft smile unveiled under a coffee-colored mustache. Hanging over the dab of hair was a long-brimmed nose, parting the man's handsome face. Two emerald green eyes smiled under bushy eyebrows glued to his large sloped forehead. He holstered his weapon as he squatted down to pull Mike to his feet, while a breeze of night air flowed through the curtains, framing the broken window. A wave of iron-scented air wafted through Mike's nostrils.

As Mike hung his head, he flicked away droplets of snot from his tear-soaked face. He felt the motley squad of cops eyeing him. After being allowed a few brief seconds to slip on his sneakers, the man quickly swept Mike into the front seat of a black unmarked cruiser, but the posse of officers remained at the house, taking photos of the crime scene. At that moment, Mike shivered from vulnerability. He was swept from his home, with nothing left of the life he knew, by a stranger.

The cop spoke softly through the brown mustache arching his top lip, "It's okay, pal. My name is Jim Miller. I'm with the Boston police. Everything will be okay." By the way Jim Miller flattened his R's, Mike surmised that the detective lived, or had lived, in North Boston. He thought about asking Jim to confirm or deny his assumption, but Mike was so absorbed in a state of shock that he could not utter one syllable. Instead, Mike closed his eyes, trying to insulate himself from the world.

Mike felt his soul die with his family. He didn't even feel the crisp breeze that blustered through the trees. He wanted to just curl up in the fetal position and rot to death. Mike studied the dark gaps between passing cars racing northbound on I-93, comparing his shambled life to the parallel emptiness pooling the waves of traffic. Mike shivered as he felt the dark gaps in his heart permanently jading his young soul. Mike felt crusty, hardened by the killing, like mountains capped by permafrost that have endured harsh climate. Mike rubbed his chest, searching for the sadness he had expected to be there, but felt nothing. His beating heart was hollow.

At the police station, Mike sat in a chair emotionlessly observing as the detective shouted back and forth with the commissioner in a heated argument. Veins bulged from either man's neck as the echoes of their yelling reverberated for miles. Detective Miller boiled with anger as he confronted the commissioner. Mike watched through the window frame in the door that led into the office of the Boston Police Commissioner. The hefty black man sat in his chair, leaning on crossed arms sitting atop his desk. Tremors surged through the blubber on his chin as the commissioner argued. Jim constantly paced back and forth in front of the man, his face blushing with clear frustration. Mike felt like a spectator watching a boxing match. Detective Miller looked back at Mike for a split-second with tender green eyes that connected with Mike's. At that moment, Mike didn't feel alone. Miller gestured wildly at the commissioner as he reached for the knob and opened the door.

"The kid's got a defect. Do you see his arm?" Jim's fatherly instincts emerged as he fought for protection for Mike. He begged the commissioner not to release this poor boy into the harsh streets of Boston, fighting other homeless wolves over scrawny meals. The vicious carnivores would eat him alive.

"Miller, look, we have to report him to DFCS. We cannot let our emotions muddle our duty. He will be in good hands," Richard Lobe, commissioner of the Boston Police Department, stated in his authoritative, "policy takes precedent" tone.

Normally, Miller would side with Lobe on the matter of resisting personal attachment while carrying out police work. In fact, officers were obligated to be objective and uninvolved. But this case was different. The boy's circumstances moved Jim but he knew Lobe was right. Mike was turned over to DFCS.

DFCS lined up therapy sessions with Dr. Riley Matthews presiding over them. After many weeks, therapists at the children's home could not help Mike heal from the incident. The psychologists tried every trick in the book to mend the damage done to his jaded heart. Every day, they had spent an hour extensively exploring his mind using techniques like word-association and other techniques which made no sense to Mike. Mike sat in a dark leather chair across from Dr. Riley Matthews, barely responding, his patience growing thin, his desire for revenge mounting.

Dr. Matthews delivered her final assessment. "I've reviewed my notes from our previous sessions," she said, staring at a notepad in her lap. She looked up and the psychologist cleared her throat before giving her prognosis. "You need a family. You need to be in a stable environment. You need a home environment. I can't do anything else," she shrugged.

Jim Miller lived in the middle-class town of Wakefield. He had a loving wife, Kathy, and two daughters whom he was wholly devoted to. For years, Jim and his wife wanted another child, a boy. When Kathy finally became pregnant, she had a miscarriage. Jim stashed that memory away in the shadows of his mind, where prescribed anti-depressants had numbed the pain and healed the wound, but there was a void in their hearts.

Miller received a call from Lobe in the early evening hours one month after DFCS took custody of Mike. Lobe told Miller that DFCS had contacted the commissioner after reviewing Dr. Matthews' psychological findings. After sharing the news with Kathy, Jim Miller drove to listen to Mathews' prognosis.

"Mike seems to need a family environment. I have done everything in my power to help him. I have tried putting him in group therapy and individual sessions and didn't see improvements. But, I think that's because he didn't connect with the others. I can't force him to interact with the group. It's like leading a horse to water." She cleared her throat. "That being said, this isn't the place for Mike. I think he would do better in a home environment where he would have a strong family-like bond with others – with you."

They drove in silence back to Wakefield. As the engine of Jim's 1977 Trans Am hummed, propelling the car sixty miles an hour on the freeway, sleep reeled Mike into a deep trance. He slid from the passenger seat back into his familiar cot as his head filled with graphic images and unnerving sounds.

He had felt warmth emitting from Laurie as she quivered in the fetal position. He remembered his heart pulsating a mile a minute. He remembered the outburst, the yelling and cursing, the shot that killed his dad came first and then, his mom's cries and pleas, and lastly, the image of Flanagan and his gang storming into his room, wrenching Laurie from his bed, and slaughtering her. Once again, blood poured through his nightmare as his world spun out of control as though in the midst of an F4 tornado...

Mike let out a powerful grunt as he awoke from the surreal dream, the life-altering catastrophe that he had suffered through only weeks ago. Cold sweat dripped from his brow as Mike looked around, trying to get his bearings. He felt oxygen escape his lungs, as if it had been chased out by Flanagan himself. Mike's drenched clothing clung to him like death. Mike gazed through weary eyes at Miller, who stared at him with a concerned expression that wrinkled his forehead. Mike did not want to be a burden to Jim, or anyone, for that matter. But the unfortunate truth was that he was. Flanagan made him this way, and Mike wanted to pay the mobster back. "You okay?" he asked.

Mike relaxed, sighed, and nodded. "Yeah." But Mike could see Jim did not buy it. It was a loaded question with ruts and unexplained, emotionally charged pits Mike didn't feel like delving into just yet. *Hell no, I'm not okay,* Mike screamed at the sound-proof walls of his mind. *All of my family is dead! No one, not even a shrink can fix that!* Emotions beyond the formation of words tore through him. He wanted to kill Flanagan. He wanted to make the persecution slow and painful. He wanted to watch the mob boss crumble in his palm. He wanted to bring Flanagan to his knees to grovel, before Mike put a bullet in his head.

The green eyes of the detective studied Mike, formulating a diagnosis like a doctor examining a patient's wounds. Shy, Mike put on a calloused shell of bravery, deflecting any inclinations toward conversation. Jim surveyed Mike for a long time. Mike stared back, watching thoughts rotate through Jim's mind. There was something Jim was keeping secret from him. Mike felt the deception between them, but did not pry.

As Jim studied him, Mike performed an overview of the hard-bitten detective. He had long, deep grooves running down his neck. When he turned his head, Mike saw, the wrinkles became more pronounced. The long years of being on the force certainly blazed a weathered complexion across Jim's face, even though he was still fairly young. Late-thirties, Mike estimated, possibly early-forties. The rest of his body was well-built, which convinced Mike he was still relatively young. No older than forty-five, Mike deduced. The car was parked in a driveway of a quaint three-story house, with levels retreating in length from bottom to top. The first story was the longest, then the second and so on. The roof jutted out, overlooking the front porch.

"Come on, I'll introduce ya to my kids," Miller said as he stepped out of the car. Mike followed him into the house and was greeted by his wife, Kathy, and their two beautiful daughters, Jessie, 10, and Katelyn, 12.

"Hi," Mike waved at Jessie, who peered at his left arm quizzically.

"What happened to your arm?"

He smiled reassuringly and explained, "Nothing. It just works differently than your arm. I was born like this." The innocence of the tiny girl's question brought a smile to Mike's dim demeanor.

The girl hugged her teddy bear and lingered quietly after that. Her thick lashes batted sleep from her glowing green eyes; a pure innocence emitted from her round face, similar to Jim's wife, Kathy.

"And this is my older daughter, Katelyn," Jim announced.

"Hello," Katelyn greeted Mike. He stared into her emerald-colored eyes, being shot in the heart by Cupid's arrow. As they grasped each other's hand, volts of electric tenderness shocked his palm.

Mike ate a supper composed of corned beef, potatoes, and cabbage with his new family members and received a new bedroom in the rear of the second floor. During supper, Mike could not take his eyes off of Katelyn. Mike lost himself in her weave of dirty blond hair. He could smell berry-flavored shampoo seeded deeply in her adorable mess of hair. Occasionally, she would catch Mike admiring her between bites of corned beef and flash a flirtatious smile back.

His heart pounded with excitement. He had experienced a feeling he had never felt before. He adored her, but he did not want to be too obvious about it. *She might be taken*, thought Mike. *Besides, who would date a cripple*, thought

Mike. He plucked Cupid's arrow from his heart and focused on the meat, silently eating. The table remained quiet throughout the rest of the meal. Mike sensed curiosity radiating from Jessie's enlarged pupils, lingering on his arm, but did not address it. He was too exhausted to recite a show-and-tell script detailing his Cerebral Palsy.

They climbed the staircase single-file. After the long day he had, Mike's legs ached with exhaustion as Kathy showed him to his new bedroom. It overlooked the small backyard, which was crammed tightly between their home and the neighbor's on the east side of the neighborhood's landscape. The green square of lawn around the perimeter of their property gave the home slightly more space; room to relax. After Kathy helped unpack the duffle bag provided by the shelter, Mike sailed into a sleep coma, once again haunted by the relentless nightmares, played over and over like a broken record. He writhed in his new mattress, tethering his legs together in a cocoon of linen.

"No!" Mike bolted upright, grappling with his surroundings, his mind trying to compute the abrupt conversion between the dream and the present. His drenched grey shirt clung to him like the Irish mob lives in the shadows of Boston. Kathy came running into the bedroom. Tears blurred his vision, rinsing the sleep from his eyes. The bed was off to the right of the window, cattycornered between two walls that came together at a right angle. The moonlight that seeped through the blinds illuminated the room casting pastel shadows. Kathy's gown glimmered as she stepped toward the soft light. Disoriented by sleep and rage, Mike glared at her through tear-filled eyes. "I'm going to catch that bastard!" he uttered sternly under his breath as strings of spittle spewed from his mouth. As Kathy knelt on the mattress, springs groaned under her moderate weight. She wrapped her arms around Mike, bringing his head to her chest. The gently comforting aura around Kathy relaxed Mike, but his heart was still frozen in a deadlock of fury.

Life continued as he returned to the false normalcy of high school. Mike grazed past the Fs in high school, earning Ds and Cs. D for depression, C for carelessness. He could not perform to the caliber of the school's expectations; in prolonged mourning, he wasn't focused on grades. But as Mike wallowed in his pit of resentment, he saw an angel that made him feel revitalized when she would float by. Her name was Katelyn. And he had taken an oath to serve as her knight in shining armor.

High school was a four-year surplus of non-applicable knowledge spewed forth from incredulous teachers. Then there was the petulant teasing from macho, hot-headed jocks. But Mike never minded their immaturity, because he knew it signaled the high school sports stars' insecurities. Until one day, the wolves began to stalk his angel.

He sat through three long, insomnia-curing lectures that day. In English, the teacher reprimanded the class for failing scores on their essays submitted the week prior. Pop quizzes in history and math carried him to lunch, a break in the day that could not arrive sooner. Mike sat by himself at lunch, nibbling his homemade sandwich, one table across from Katelyn, watching her talk to friends. It made him smile when she revealed her pearl-white teeth.

Mike had become a loner. Ever since he was orphaned, he distanced himself from the ones dearest to him, including Jim, Kathy, Jesse and Katelyn. Mike locked his foster family out, afraid that Flanagan would come for them next. And so, he monitored Katelyn from a distance as she mingled with her girlfriends. Katelyn was independent; it was one of the many qualities he admired, other than her beauty and smarts.

While pondering this, he observed three broad-shouldered jocks stroll toward Katelyn and the other girls. He recognized them as Will Newham, star-quarterback, Keith Dublin, full-back, and Arnold Elroy, starting tight-end. Newham flashed a smile at Katelyn; he leaned in to whisper something in her ear. The emerald green eyes flashed a look of astonishment as she slid uncomfortably in her seat.

The crashing black waves of hair atop Newham's head glistened in the panels of florescent lights of the cafeteria. He wore a tight white shirt and jeans that outlined his chiseled physique like a second layer of skin. A light stubble of whiskers concealed red bumps of acne. As the hulk rested his dense forearms on the table, a terrible smile sprawled across his unkempt face. Katelyn's face morphed into a look of disgust. She moved away when the Neanderthal caught her arm.

Flinching, Mike put his sandwich down, intently watching the scene unfold. He debated whether she needed rescuing or not. *Relax*, he breathed deeply and unclenched his fists. He knew Katelyn was defiant towards predators and maintained her guard. But some innate feeling stroked his scalp, indicating Katelyn was in a shark tank and out of her depth. He waited, muscles tense with anticipation. He watched the bum snatch her hand and haul her in to his lips.

Mike sprang from his seat and tore down the aisle between tables. Flames of anger burned inside him as he raced toward Katelyn's antagonist. "Hey, fuckhead!" Mike yelled at Newham. The grease ball turned, looking at Mike with deadpan eyes. "Leave the girl alone!"

The jock snorted, "What do you mean? I ain't bothering her." Newham stood in front of the posse that engulfed Katelyn. Mike stuck his thumb over his shoulder, gesturing for Katelyn to move away from Newham. Positioning himself between the dense wall of muscle and Katelyn, Mike said, "Get out of here before I break your nose." The jock leaned his head back and laughed. "Ah, man. This is priceless," he said to his followers.

Mike's blood boiled at the snide remark. "I said get out of here."

"Make me." The grease-ball shoved Mike backwards a few paces. Mike clenched his jaw, ready to clobber Newham when Katelyn stepped between them. The grease-ball's black pupils scowled at Mike, as they locked glares. A crowd slowly gathered around them. Katelyn dug a bony elbow into Mike's side and shot him a reassuring look. *It's fine*, the gesture said, her vibrant stare transcended his boiling rage. A boy then appeared from a clump of students and intervened, helping Katelyn usher Mike from the pack of roguish wolves through the crowd of on-lookers.

Baffled, Mike was not able to form words. He and the boy navigated a stream of bodies walking down the hallway. As they rounded a corner, Mike broke free from the boy's firm grasp. Mike massaged his arm where the boy held him, ruminating about the unnecessary rescue. They darted into a small alcove enclosed by a pair of rusting doors, when Mike caught his breath to speak. "What the hell, man?!" Mike boomed, embarrassed.

"Cool off, boss." The boy raised his hands in submission. His voice was slathered in the unmistakable whine of a Southie accent. "You're lucky. I saved you from a beat down. Not to mention a few days of suspension. But don't thank me," he calmly retorted. Mike sighed. The boy was right. Mike would have been suspended for starting the altercation, which then would postpone his graduation for at least half of a semester. He surveyed the skinny young man who wore a black AC/DC short-sleeve t-shirt with black jeans and black Converse sneakers. His hair was combed back over his scalp in a mullet. In his dark pupils, insanity flickered. A mark was noticeable on the side of his neck, shading the rim of his right ear. It was a tattoo made up of a series of intersecting spades.

Mike tore away from the mysterious boy to look at his arm which had begun to swell. Dull pain sank in and began to strangle Mike's bicep. He grimaced when he poked at the bulbous patch of purple. A door squeaked open, letting in the echo of footsteps that tapped down the corridor. Mike looked up, watching a slender silhouette cast over him. His heart raced as an elated feeling rushed through him. Katelyn appeared from the shadows as Mike heard the bell ring. Her angelic presence deafened talkative crowds of teenagers pushing past them.

"You okay?" Katelyn asked as she strode over to him.

"Fine," Mike replied, shaking off the last bit of pain not engulfed by numbness. He walked past Katelyn and flashed a reassuring smile at her. She did not return the gesture. "Please don't stick up for me again. It'll only get you in trouble." She said in a stern tone.

Mike shook his head. "But, that guy, he…" Rage welled in the back of his throat, causing him to stumble over his words. Mike wanted another chance to bash the obnoxious jockey's brains in. *That might be the perfect solution*, Mike mulled.

"I know," Katelyn softly mumbled under her breath before spearing Mike with her green eyes. She held his gaze, those emeralds glaring at him, "He's a jerk. That's for sure. He's like that to everyone." Katelyn flashed warm smile and affectionately rubbed Mike's arm. Mike turned weak at her slightest touch, like putty in her hands. He smiled back as she turned and strode down the hall. Katelyn had somehow summoned the power to kill the pain. He went back to pay the boy an apology for his boorish behavior but the alcove was desolate. The tattooed boy had evaporated into thin air, disappearing into the shadows, reappearing in the next decade.

Alistair Creasy was born into a league of shadows. He knew when to be present and when to melt away. It was time for him to disappear. Creasy was a member of a secret organization, a cult, with the desire to establish a new world order by overturning bureaucracies, eliminating power-drunk politicians and bringing more power to the people. A revolution was coming and Creasy would be on the front line; but not yet. The cult still needed thousands more followers for the rebellion and recruitment was slow.

The cult leadership had assigned Creasy to keep tabs on Mike. He dug in his pockets for change as he walked toward a phone booth; seventy-five cents was cradled in the soft fabric. He slid the door shut, dropped the change into the slot and dialed the number.

A scraggly voice answered the on the other end, "Yes?"

"He's here." His nasally Southie accent reverberating through the phone booth like a Super Ball. The booth was cramped. Creasy could feel his body heat steaming the booth like a sauna. This had been the first time he had made contact with his elders since the inception of his new plan, and he grew nervous thinking of how he would present it. It was for the better, Creasy reminded himself. Static exploded in his ear as the voice crackled on the line.

"Good. Have you tried to persuade him yet?"

"No. I want to try to catch a bigger fish." He grew even more nervous but he knew he could hook dozens of followers with the idea as he continued, "I think we would be better off with the Irish mob."

"The mob?" exclaimed the voice.

"Yes. We would be able to gain plenty of followers with one swoop. Permission to proceed?" Hollow static echoed through the receiver as Creasy bit his lip. He hoped his leader could foresee the rewards his alternative plan offered.

After listening to perpetual howls of white noise from the line, Creasy decided to abandon the offer when, finally, the voice ruptured the maze of static. "Permission granted," the voice mumbled as he terminated the call. A smile unfolded across Creasy's face as he placed the receiver in its cradle and exited the booth.

For sixteen years Mike had dreamed of having that momentous opportunity of challenging Flanagan to a duel. He fantasized toting a pistol, squaring off with the mob boss, and lodging a bullet in his head. Mike endured years of sorrow and anger, unable to bury the burdens that stalked him night and day, wading in the shadows of his mind, casting tales of sinister thoughts of revenge in his mind. Now, twenty-eight years old, he continued to wait for that fantastic moment of vengeance. As he stood behind the McDonald's counter, Mike also pondered about Alistair Creasy, the boy who intervened and prevented an all-out brawl in the high school cafeteria. Creasy eventually found Mike and a tenable friendship formed.

With nothing except a high-school diploma under his belt, Mike commanded the cash register where he silently reflected upon the roads that led him to this bland lifestyle. He had barely graduated from high school, which had deterred Mike from seeking higher education. One by one, the small group of close friends Mike had been acquainted with split, blazing different paths and acquiring different lifestyles. Katelyn, college-bound, shipped off to MIT where she would adopt computer science as her niche. Orientated to the other end of the spectrum, far less academically motivated, Mike found his way to this current job and his seemingly only friend, Creasy.

"There's no good job out there." Creasy said, staring at the ground. Mike nodded, half-listening. "My friend is doing something called an enlightenment workshop. It sounds cool."

"What is an enlightenment workshop?" Mike asked.

"Don't know." Creasy shrugged. "But, it's better than nothing."

An eerie sensation billowed from Mike's chest but his interest was piqued. He agreed to accompany Creasy to a meeting

Creasy, like Mike, had experience navigating the rough areas of Southie.

Unlike Mike, he had little choice but to learn ways to survive on the tough streets. For most of Creasy's life, he watched cops do more harm than good. He knew the influence Boston's finest had and the fear and pain they had inflicted on the poor. He had decided that they simply wielded too much power, and he wanted to help change that.

Just as Mike witnessed the brutal deaths of his family by the Irish mob boss, Creasy remembered the night his parents were beaten to death by Boston pigs. His father was merely a pastor at Saint Bridge Parish. Creasy awoke to the beating and panicked. His heart palpitated as he raced to ward off the cops, but it was too late. By the time Creasy had reached his father, the cops had left him in a pool of blood. His father outstretched his arm feebly and took Creasy's hand and murmured one word. "Cross." Creasy scrambled to his father's bedside table and took the pocket-size cross his father carried around. He hurried back to the pool of blood and slid the cross into his father's hand. His heart ached as he watched the life drain from his father's face.

Just as Mike found his foster dad, Jim Miller, Creasy eventually found a guardian of sorts, a "mentor". Like Miller, the "mentor" gave Creasy a new life, providing food, shelter and guidance. Unlike Miller, the "mentor" was no saint.

Creasy grew weary as he squinted at the bright computer screen. He had a long day of checking the backgrounds of new cult initiates for the "mentor". In addition to doing background checks, Creasy was a field agent of sorts. He had recently staked out the Irish mob in an empty O'Kitty's pub that resided in the stronghold of Southie. He was the inside man, tracking the mob and reporting their business to his "mentor", all this leading up to his new initiative of the cult succeeding the Irish mob in Southie.

Creasy became increasingly fascinated by death. Ways to die, ways to kill, it was an all-encompassing hobby. Followers of his blog, potential cult initiates, raved about his postings online. Creasy hurried to finish his report on Mike so that he could indulge his hobby. Creasy connected with his mentor inside a chat room.

Mentor: How is the plan going?

Creasy: Well.

Mentor: Report?

Creasy: Done. Faxing it to you now.

Creasy smiled as he placed the report in the fax. He punched "the mentor's" fax number on the machine's keypad and pressed FAX. The leaves of paper were slowly ingested by the machine, one by one. As he waited for "the mentor's" acknowledgement to pop up on his computer screen, he thought about Mike.

People like Mike made good cult members; people who had a traumatic childhood and/or harbored angry feelings created by traumatic incidents. Creasy knew this from personal experience and sympathized with Mike. Alistair knew Mike needed as much support as he could find. The cult was like a family. They acted as a unit with unquestioning commitment for each other and for their leader. The cult forbids any discrimination, welcoming individuals from all walks of life and offered bountiful guidance. They found careers for the members that paid good money. They provided counseling and group therapy sessions for the ones who needed it. Everything that had helped Alistair would also help Mike. Alistair also knew Mike wanted to avenge his family by killing Flintlock Flanagan – a job that the cult could take care of.

Sirens echoed from the alley outside the McDonald's on Commonwealth Avenue as dusk stifled the sun. Mike peered through the massive panes of glass, watching flickering strobes of red and blue shuttle by. The ear-piercing sounds shook the glass as Mike stepped behind it, curious to see the cause of the brigade of Crown Victoria's. Mike looked on as tires screeched to a halt, unloading a miniature army of cops clutching pistols at their hips.

The brigade was instantly swallowed by a barrage of gunfire as the squad rushed into the Bank of America from their cruisers. The intoxicating odor of burning rubber waivered from their cruisers, as six rounds rang in Mike's ears, moments after the cops disappeared. A crowd of four wearing ape masks dashed from the scene, firing rounds at the cops, picking them off, one by one. Mike's heart raced as the ape masks ran toward the McDonald's. He rushed to lock the entrance, and then dove behind the counter.

A co-worker named Donnie emerged from the back. She looked at him, befuddled. He put a finger to his mouth and whispered, "Get down!" But, before she could react, blood poured through her chest. Stunned, Mike caught her as she fell to the floor. Blood spurted from her left breast, as Mike put pressure on the wound. Panicking, Mike cursed as he scrambled to his knees, laying Donnie on the tiled floor.

"Shit!" Mike bent over Donnie, watching her shocked face grow deathly pale. Blood spurted on his face as he tried to prevent more from erupting from the wound. The slime ran through his fingers in diverting rivers. He tapped her wrist with his crippled left hand trying to find her pulse. "Hang in there, Don." He finally caught her faint heart-beat. It was rapidly dying. A brick of sadness crashed into him as he began to cry for help. He switched hands and frantically fumbled for his cell phone to call 911.

A dispatcher calmly answered. "Nine-one-one, what's your emergency?"

"My friend has been shot," Mike frantically said as life painfully dissolved through the cracks of his hands. The pool of red dispersed in a wide arch, coating the tiles, like the black plague. He felt the undertow of death drag Donnie under the chaotic surf as a stab of fear speared him in the back.

"Where are you located?" the dispatcher asked.

"McDonald's. 540 Commonwealth Avenue. She was shot by a bank robber. Hurry."

Mike stood in shock next to a Crowne Vic, recounting the shooting as it had unfolded to a cop recording witness recollections of the surreal scene. Blood stains drenched his McDonald's uniform and made his shirt sag. He cringed as he felt the unbearable weight of death clinging to him. Mike ignored the mammoth yellow double arches looming over him. Shivers rolled up his spine, as he saw Donnie's deadpan stare fixed on him. Mike was unable to shake the eerie feeling grasping his back, gnawing at his mind. He would remind himself to put his two-week notice in as soon as possible.

As the detective concluded his questions, Jim appeared from the shadows of vehicles swarming the parking lot. By Jim's casual dress, Levi jeans and dusty bomber jacket, Mike knew he was off-duty. Jim walked toward Mike who was instantly cuffed with Jim's concerned apprehension.

"You okay?" he asked.

Mike felt Jim's intimidating green eyes gently observing his reaction. "Fine," his hollow voice replied. "I don't want to come back here," he whispered.

Jim paused, and then asked, "What are you thinking?"

Mike cleared his throat, as apprehension tickled the back. "I hate feeling helpless, I need to help stop shit like this. I want to be a police officer."

Vicious snarls echoed from the blood-sprayed brick as Gomez traveled through the maze of corridors, carrying pockets full of heroin and syringes. The shadows scaling the brick above him growled at each other, sinking their fangs into fur and flesh, wrestling to the death. Cheers welled after the abrupt cessation of bestial sneers from the four-legged contenders. Gomez stood at the edge of the bloody battlefield, curious to see who won. The contender stood triumphantly over the champ, grasping a chunk of flesh between his robust jaws like a cigar. Cult members darted into the center of the small makeshift arena to drag the loser's carcass aside. A fresh smear of blood stained the dark landscape, trailing from the dog's carcass. The rest of Creasy's flock gathered around the winner preparing the pit bull for the next round of fighting.

Gomez stood next to Creasy and smiled. "Good, si?"

"Si, Señor Gomez," Creasy responded. "Tiene los elementos (*Do you have the items*)?" Creasy's campaign of gathering followers spread through cartels of drug-dealers.

"Si," Gomez replied as he extracted the needles and heroin from his pocket.

Creasy slipped him a wad of currency. "Muchos gracias, Señor."

Hernando Gomez felt an irritating sensation gouging his stomach making deals with Creasy, but he had no choice. He had refused once before. In return, his wife and daughter had vanished. Creasy led a league of shadows. The shadows were at his command. And they stole his family. When it happened, Gomez was on his route dealing with customers, too busy to tend to Creasy's needs. Upon returning from his trip, Gomez came home to an empty wreck that had once been his home. His family had been abducted by Creasy's cult, as Gomez had discovered via a phone call from Creasy.

"They're fine," Creasy had reassured Gomez as tears streaked down his face. Gomez felt pitiful and weak, weeping over the phone. His salty tears reflected in his voice as he wrenched the invisible knife from his heart. "Just do as I say and your family will be returned to you." Thus, Gomez became Creasy's pawn.

Suddenly, a vociferous growl followed by a cracking sound and shouting of obscenities interrupted Gomez's thoughts. Brutish snarls intensified as the throng of cult members charged, shoving Gomez against a brick wall, slamming his head into the gritty fabric. As he dropped to the ground, Gomez's hand felt at the wound in the back of his head and the warm blood trickling through his fingers. The world spun like a dreidel as Gomez's eyes rolled back into his skull and his brain rattled in its protective casing as he hit the ground cold. All the while, druggies and drunkards frantically dispersed through the narrow alley.

Over the next several weeks, Alistair Creasy watched the cult grow. He mined through rebel gangs, from which he had gathered thirty followers. In hindsight, Creasy figured he could polish up his speeches. So, he reworked his introduction, coming up with a better attention-grabber, establishing the mission, and ending with gusto. That did the trick. After a while, Creasy recognized what made criminals tick. The recruitment had been slow at first, but after digging deeper and making connections in Boston's underground world of criminals, Creasy had hit the jackpot. He pulled out all the stops; drugs, money, and the promise of eternal life.

Meanwhile, Mike's nightmares continued to haunt him but they were becoming less vivid, leaving him with a feeling of residual fear. Mike watched the darkness drift in the air like marshmallows in gelatin. *Get up*, Mike heard his conscience usher. *Get up and go for a run.* Mike obeyed. He shuffled to his dresser and snatched some rarely-worn sweatpants and a sweatshirt. He then opened the top drawer and extracted an ashy undershirt. After brushing sleep from his eyes, Mike took the garments to the bathroom. Downstairs, Mike slipped on his socks and tattered Nike sneakers. *The highlight of my day*, Mike mused sarcastically. He pulled up the tongue and double-knotted the laces.

Satisfied that the sneakers fit like gloves, Mike strode to the door where he was met by Jim. The middle-aged man was decked out in running attire. Jim's trimmed yet muscular figure glowed in the darkness because of the reflective running shorts. He also wore a dry-weave sleeveless top and a Nike mesh visor, emulating a model posing for a photographer for Runner's World. Mike laughed.

"What?" Jim asked as if he missed the punchline to a joke.

"Nothing." Mike responded.

"You ready?" Jim asked, obviously changing the subject.

"Yeah." Mike responded tersely.

Jim led the way through darkened rooms of the colonial home to the bright outside world. The sun peeped through the trees and over rooftops as Jim pressed his palms into the brick siding of the house and extended his legs, loosening his lean calf muscles. After a ten-minute stretch, they trotted down the empty neighborhood street. Because of Mike's poor fitness, the run rapidly morphed into a torturous undertaking. His scrawny joints trembled with every step. After a mile of agony, Mike's lungs and legs burned. Sweat stung his eyes, transforming the landscape around him into a French impressionist painting, enriched by deep, fully-drawn waves of orange and yellow background. Trying to blot out the discouraging failure of running, Mike breathed deeply, letting the fresh, morning air soothe his burning lungs.

Jim walked effortlessly back to their home, only slightly winded by the run, while Mike sucked wind and winced from the discomfort caused by his tightly-strung leg muscles. Talons of pain dug into the meaty balls of his foot; *damn, I need to get different shoes if I'm gonna be serious about this.* As Mike lumbered sorely through the garage entrance, Kathy's voice sung throughout their home. Mike flexed his facial muscles into a thin, painful smile.

Jim's footsteps followed Mike while the fragrance of sweat followed both. Jim walked into the master suite's bathroom and closed the door. Mike heard the water being turned on as he headed to his room in the rear of the house. He eased himself up on his bed where he peeled his socks off. Pain exploded from the bottom of Mike's foot.

"Fuck!" Mike muttered. The dead skin was slowly ripping from his heel, revealing a cherry-red patch of skin. Mike held his breath as he gingerly peeled blades of dead skin. A burning sensation scorched the oval of raw flesh. He was about to bellow a moan but then heard the phone being slammed into its console. Excited feet darted up the stairs. A loud exuberant set of knocks slammed into his door.

"Come in." Mike called to the knock, stifling his cry of pain as he peeled the other sock off. He could feel the cotton fibers fuse with the opened wound. The air stung the opened wound, bringing tears to Mike's eyes.

Kathy entered. "Hi." Her bright smile turned into a dark frown. "OH, boy. Those are wicked blisters. Let me see if we have something for those. Then I'll tell you the good news." Kathy disappeared from the bedroom.

Muted by a cloud of weariness, and utterly dissatisfied by his stamina, he muttered, "Great." *Can hardly wait* he thought.

Kathy returned with a small bottle of Bactine, a box of sterilized bandages, and a thick roll of medical tape.

Mike sprawled out on the bed and hung his feet over the foot of the bed. He assumed the position to be properly bandaged. He lay on his stomach so the Bactine wouldn't drip. He gasped when the cold liquid drained into his wounds, stinging them. "Shit!" Mike gasped through clenched teeth as the prickly feeling of snipping hermit crabs invaded his heels. To get his mind off of his predicament, he asked Kathy "So, what's the good news?"

"Oh, yeah." Kathy said after tapping her chin with her index finger, thinking. "So, Katelyn is coming home from BC! I just got off the phone with her."

Mike felt her swath the gauze around his tender heel, then urge the fiber to conform to his heel. He winced once more as grains of pain impounded his foot. "Great! How long is she staying?" Mike asked, eager to see his angel again.

"Um, she didn't say," Kathy replied. "You know Katelyn flies by the seat of her pants."

"True," Mike acknowledged, remembering his angel's whimsical planning. He smiled widely as he recalled one of their infamous midnight expeditions to Wakefield Bowladrome where they wagered on who could bowl the most points in ten minutes. Knowing neither of them were good bowlers, Mike reluctantly had agreed to the challenge.

He had bowled a measly sixty. Katelyn triumphantly had racked up a staggering ninety-five. Katelyn had laughed and roasted Mike's inept bowling skills, while Mike just enjoyed being with Katelyn. A fool in love, he could not help but smile at that memory as it rippled through his mind.

Kathy finished bandaging Mike's blistering feet.

"There. Is that okay?"

"Yeah, thanks." Mike nodded. He stood from the bed, striding a few paces across the room. But, the cushioning around his injured heel did not register as he was still lost in thought about Katelyn's homecoming. The soft bandage caressed his heel as gently as Katelyn's green eyes embraced his heart.

Flanagan entered the safe house back room of Cask N'Flaggan where his mob affiliates patiently waited, chit-chatting in low monotones. As he rubbed his greying whiskers, he mentally rehearsed his resignation speech. He was old. His career was slowly crumbling about him. He was running out of facets of immunity from the FBI's Upper Echelon Program and sensed that he would soon be wrung out and hung to dry.

Flanagan took his seat at the head of the table and cleared his scratchy throat. "My run as the head of the mob is nearing its end, gentlemen," he admitted. "It's been a hellava couple of decades." He paused to wait for the scattered applause to subside. Flanagan flashed a brief smile and continued. "Good years," Flanagan said, seducing his captivated audience and easing the pending uproar his retirement would inevitably cause. Flanagan peered at the dozens of eyes staring at him in disbelief. "But the cops are closing in on us, and it is too much. It's a different world. I have out lived my effectiveness. We need to regroup and reorganize. We need to disappear while we can."

"Wait, why disappear?" O'Flaherty objected. "What about our immunity? I thought we'd be protected if we got caught? We turned on some of our guys, they're not gonna forget that if they ever get out of prison. The FBI needs to help us disappear. You promised us the program would work for us."

"And it will if we keep our heads low and leave Boston. The cops can't follow us out of state; it's not in their jurisdiction. They would need the FBI's help and the FBI will honor the Echelon Program and leave us alone," Flanagan tried to calm O'Flaherty's rage.

"I got two kids, a wife who spends like a fiend, and no resume. What the fuck do you expect me to do? Package groceries?!" O'Flaherty retorted.

"Disappear," Flanagan demanded. He could sense mutiny building among his constituents. "I can get you fake passports. You leave the state, the country, go to Mexico, go where ever you want. Just don't stay here."

"Mexico?! Give me a fucking break!" The infectious outburst spread through the room. Flanagan felt a migraine come on. He buried his head in his palms as his skull pounded with carving pain. Several pulsations rattled his mind, as if footsteps were trampling his head to a pulp. It was not until he felt the tremors spiral up his elbow that he realized the pulsations were emitted by an outside source.

When the vibrations ceased, Flanagan peered toward a dark figure looming over the corner of the table. The blade of a knife glimmered against a backdrop of black. The figure was that of a lanky man, dressed in black from head to foot. Goosebumps pimpled from Flanagan's neck as an eerie coldness emanated from the man in black.

Concealing his anticipated foreboding with a solemn, unimpressed look, Flanagan asked the stranger, "Who the hell are you?"

"I am Alistair Creasy. I have a proposition," the nasally voice responded.

A Southie accent, Flanagan noted. For the first time in his life, Flanagan was reticent. All of his authority had been wrenched from him when the room plunged into cold darkness as the figure tranquilly paced the floor. The knife blade recoiled behind the man's black sleeve.

"What proposition?" Flanagan's voice trailed off.

"I can give you and your men complete protection if you join my cause; to rebel against the oppressive grip of law enforcement and government. Our Founding Fathers guaranteed an independent nation run by the people, of the people, and for the people. But, instead of adhering to their wishes, the people are lied to and used as bargaining tools to satisfy their greed and desire for celebrity!"

Falling captive to the formidable yet unnatural tone, Flanagan's mobsters cheered as ominous feelings tore through Flanagan's own gut. Flanagan was stunned by how fast things had spiraled out of control. He bit his lip and remained uncomfortably silent as he witnessed his men becoming mesmerized by the man's rant.

"We must act now, my friends!" Creasy shouted, throwing a triumphant fist in the air. His words were so bold, so brazen, they were spitting like fire. Up until this point, Flanagan believed he was the alpha among his fellow criminals and that his word was the pep-talk mobsters needed. At some point it was. But, much like him, Flanagan's leadership had lost its luster. These new-age gangsters apparently wanted something more – something Creasy had. In Creasy's eyes, Flanagan could see the fire spread. It was madness. "We must unite, we must fight!"

As Creasy talked with his new recruits, Flanagan and five others, ditched the manic scene but not before Flanagan met the stare of Creasy's black, cold, soulless eyes. *Brainwashed*, thought Flanagan, *just like he's doing to my men.* Flanagan could tell Creasy was a rabid dog on an irrational mission, who must be stopped. As he strode away, Flanagan rubbed his chin, pondering how Creasy could be stopped. All of his cards had been dealt … except for one.

The day melted into night. The time spent with Katelyn was anything except wasted. Mike was in a dreamland. He had felt his world spinning ever since Katelyn had returned from MIT, careening a shockwave of love into his chest. Mike had been reborn. His heart floated higher and higher, as the moon rose to its pinnacle in the midnight-blue sky shining above them: the perfect backdrop for the canopy of shining stars.

"I like Boston at night," Mike commented as they strolled down the sidewalk, hearing the echoing click of the bowling alley's doors. "Kind of peaceful."

"Yeah," Katelyn yawned as she rested her head on Mike's shoulder. He liked carrying the extra ten pounds. It was comforting. During the day, Katelyn was her own watchdog – she was independent, her best quality in Mike's opinion. But, being this close to Katelyn, Mike could absorb her softness as she let him be her protector. The weight embraced his inner strength. It made him feel invincible. He happily watched his angel close her eyes as berry shampoo wafted through his nose. They strolled back to Katelyn's car, when a pebble skipped across the sidewalk. Mike turned around, and saw the pancake-flat contour of a Fedora brim peaking from behind the Cask N'Flaggan Irish pub.

"Hey," the shadow hiding under the hat breathed, waving his fingers under the cold shadows. Mike recognized Flanagan, as he tilted the Fedora up at an acute angle. Like an overly aggressive pit bull, Mike quickly pushed Katelyn toward her car.

"Wait for me in the car," he told Katelyn in an agitated growl. He ignored Katelyn's baffled stare as he walked into the shadows, staring straight at Flanagan, wanting to unleash holy hell on him.

Mike took no notice of Katelyn's reluctant footsteps as her shadow followed her walking against the gritty backdrop of the asphalt. He waited until he heard the secure lock of her midnight blue Saturn sedan before shoving Flanagan.

"What the hell do you want?!" Mike shouted. He felt a fury of rage crawl up his spine looking at a ghost of the man that killed his family.

"I need your help. I need to talk to Miller." the man replied. "Why the fuck would I want to help you?! I'd just as soon kill your ass!" Mike's voice was stifled as the barrel of Flanagan's pistol stunned him. He gulped down his words, as Flanagan began speaking in a quiet, but unyielding tenor.

"I need help," Flanagan reiterated. "There's somebody who is a threat to all of us, to the city, to the state, to the US, to everyone." Flanagan shot a quick, piercing glance at Mike that speared another spike of foreboding through his ribs.

From then on, Mike smothered any urge to interrupt Flanagan's tale of Creasy. Flanagan recounted the day that Creasy had converted Flanagan's outfit of renegades as he and a few of his loyal dogs fled from the uproar Creasy had conducted. When Flanagan concluded, Mike gave him an incredulous glance, but then reeled it back in, when he reviewed the tale through his mind. *Sounds like Creasy*, Mike told himself as he nodded.

Flanagan continued, "Tell the cops. Your adoptive father is a cop, right?" Mike paused as he felt a daunting chill blast his skin.

"How did you know?" Mike swallowed his bewilderment, slightly embarrassed.

"I'm the Irish mob, kid," Flanagan responded, chuckling. "I'm supposed to know."

As Flanagan spoke, Mike noticed his sheepish behavior. The way Flanagan talked in a tone slightly above a whisper. The way he nervously wrung his hands – all indications of a paranoid man being watch. As Mike was distracted by the signals Flanagan was sending him, he had forgotten who Flintlock Flanagan was and his tenuous correspondences within law-enforcement. Flanagan could probably recite the names of Boston detectives backwards. Mike looked away from Flanagan and peered around the corner where Katelyn waited, watching the street as two cars quietly breezed by. He considered her safety if he didn't take Flanagan's forewarning seriously. Flanagan, being as intertwined as he was in organized crime, had potential of being a forthcoming, trustworthy informant. But, by the same token, he could be setting them up.

"How can I trust you?" Mike jabbed as he spun back to face Flanagan.

"You can't." Flanagan clearly stated, smiling. He stepped closer to Mike, his peevish grin melted to an honest, pure look of grave concern. "But, you have to. Tell the cop – your adopted father – that I will come in willingly as an Echelon participant. He'll know what that means." With that, he submerged back into the shadows as instantly as he sprang from them. Trying to decipher Flanagan's cryptic message for Jim, Mike walked to Katelyn's car.

"What was that?" Katelyn asked.

"Uh… Nothing." Mike responded distantly. Still sensing the presence of someone lurking in the shadows, Mike glanced back into the black labyrinth from which Flanagan surfaced, searching for answers. Why should he help his arch nemesis?

Mike and Katelyn returned home from their date, after the smooth-going evening was spoiled by Flanagan. They crept into their bedrooms and bid each other goodnight. Mike wondered if they would seal their night out with a kiss. But, much to his chagrin, he read Katelyn's motion as a no. Mike watched her tread to her bedroom before plunging into his, concentrating on Flanagan's warning. He could not erase the appearance Flanagan made from his restless mind. What did he mean by, "A threat to everyone?" Could he have meant a threat to everyone in Boston? Massachusetts? The world? The vagueness of Flanagan's claim worried Mike. He closed his eyes and tried to clear his head, but instead drifted into morbid dreams of Flanagan and Creasy going toe to toe – their poses waging a war.

His heartbeat quickened as he tossed and turned in bed, fighting both Flanagan and Creasy. Mike stood in the middle of the feud, watching both gangs tear each other apart as blood coated the city and sky surrounding them. Emerging from his dream state, Mike looked around the room and, through the cracked door, caught a glimpse of Katelyn rush into the bathroom, her crinkled, golden hair fluttering behind her as she slammed the door shut. Mike sighed, feeling his heart slamming itself against the walls of his chest.

Moments later, Katelyn emerged from the bathroom as Mike sat on the edge of the bed. Their eyes met and, by the way Katelyn's eyebrows clashed, he knew Katelyn sensed his uneasiness. She stepped into his bedroom as he collected himself. Taking deep, cleansing breaths, Mike ran his fingers through his matted brown hair and wiped the sweat from his forehead. As Katelyn folded one long leg on the mattress, Mike felt her emerald eyes burning in the side of his head, begging the question, "What's wrong?"

"Nightmares."

Mike sighed, knowing that there was no way of avoiding the grim subject. "Of him."

Katelyn nodded, acknowledging that she knew who he was referring to. She sat with one leg crossed under the other, which dangled loosely off the bed. Mike gazed at her slender silhouette, as the bad thoughts evaporated from his mind. Her black tank-top caressed every curvature of her torso, and a red pair of Sophie's wrapped around her thin hips, skirting her lean upper-thighs. Every time Mike looked at her, he could feel the griminess of his sorrow washed away. She extended a soft, soothing hand and gently squeezed his shoulder, consoling Mike. Immediately, her warm presence melted the cold nightmares that filled his mind. She lay next to him.

The barrel of Flanagan's Beretta still loomed in his mind and Mike knew the aging man he had bumped into that evening was the same bastard he was too familiar with. He still loathed the crook for what he had done, but something about Flanagan's request help casted a different light on the situation.

Flanagan's voice, though soft, was still commanding. He seemed sincere and very concerned with a potentially powerful threat. Still, Mike had witnessed what Flanagan was capable of, and feared that history would repeat itself. These thoughts were suffocating Mike, as he mentally debated whether he should assist the old Irish mobster in winning back his outfit, or let Flanagan spar with Creasy to determine who runs the muscle in Boston.

Annoyed with this dilemma, Mike got up to get dressed and whispered to Katelyn, "I need air. Would you like to come for a walk?" Katelyn looked away and rubbed a speck of sleep from her eye with her petite finger. "Sure. Let me get dressed."

Mike slid into denim jeans and a short-sleeved, forest-green shirt with a Fighting Irish logo on the back. Long, snarling snores filtered out from Kathy and Jim's bedroom, indicating they were in a deep slumber. Mike stuffed the hand-me-down cellular phone into his jeans' pocket in case Jim or Kathy woke up to discover two empty beds and began panicking. They snaked downstairs and out the front door. Katelyn locked the door and slipped the key into her front jeans' pocket.

The skin on the bottom of Mike's feet had almost completely healed. The soft flesh on the bottom of his heels had reformed a new layer of skin and, even though the blisters had not yet entirely disappeared from his feet, Mike strolled comfortably in the his New Balances, that were now fitted with gel-insoles. Katelyn and Mike walked out of the neighborhood and onto Chestnut Street, walking side-by-side, with almost-corresponding strides. They remained under a blanket of silence, smiling, enjoying each other's company. The night was cool and refreshing. Only the moon watched over them as they turned onto North Avenue when Katelyn asked Mike why he wanted to be a cop.

"Who told you about that?" Mike asked, stunned that Katelyn knew.

"Dad," she replied. Then, she turned back to the question. "Why put your life on the line?"

"Because it feels right." Mike replied. Mike wanted to share his deepest thoughts. He wanted Katelyn to understand the journey that led him to this burning desire of his. And he wanted her to support him and to know the insidious circumstance that drove him to his decision.

"I grew up in South Boston. There was a lot of crime, a lot of gangs and drugs. Innocent people would get robbed by some neighborhood gang or worse," Mike said, remembering the many nights he heard or witnessed people getting mugged. Mike continued as his mind fast-forwarded to the night Flanagan barged into his home. Mike's face burned with anger. He could still see his sister's blood staining his bedroom walls. "Guess I'm just tired of seeing bad stuff happen to good people. I want to prevent criminals from preying on the vulnerable. There are a lot of freaks out there who do things."

"Like what happened to you." The smoking barrel of Flanagan's gun entered his mind, conjuring a grimmer feeling inside. *Prevent unforgivable deeds*, thought Mike.

"Yes," he answered gravely. Mike knew the monster that lurked inside him, and knew it would not rest until he could somehow quench his thirst for revenge. He didn't want anybody else to have these feelings. *They could drive you insane*, Mike thought.

"Very noble of you, acting like a knight in shining armor," she commented, winking.

He could not keep from smiling. Somehow, Katelyn sang the perfect words to the perfect beat, coaxing Mike with her charm. Mike stopped walking, enthralled with the golden glow of the angel beside him. Her eyes twinkled. Those eyes, inviting him to kiss her. As his heart thumped in his chest, Mike felt her warmth and caressed her face. He closed his eyes as he tasted her beauty. He leaned back, allowing her to come up for air, awaiting a response. She blushed, grinning from ear to ear. He wondered how she thought this first kiss was when rustles whirled in the darkness.

The whimpering sound of an injured animal echoed in a nearby alley. Mike and Katelyn crept cautiously toward the noise. A robust shadow crawled to them. As they crept closer, the woozy figure abruptly collapsed in the dark backstreet.

"Mike," Kate hollered as she stooped beside the animal. "I think his hind leg his broken." As they checked the injured dog, Mike felt another presence in the long narrow alley. He moved quickly but cautiously as he scanned the darkness, an eerie chill ran up his spine. He felt a presence pass, then heard an approaching car engine abruptly die. Keys jingled with the casual thump of boots. Mike's heart rocketed through his throat. He advanced three long strides and stepped in front of Katelyn, protecting her from the evil that smiled at him.

"Hello, Mike." The shadow spoke in a nerve-rattling Southie accent. "We meet again."

Mike's mind warped through the past, instantaneously replaying a chapter that had been written back in high school when Creasy had befriended him. Memories of the lanky boy he had known conjured a cycle of photographs that spun through his mind in snippets. Mike's heart surged through rapid beats as he recalled the commencement of their tenuous friendship.

As he took in the dark man standing before him, Mike was unable to link the teenage Creasy he had known to the portentous creature standing in front of him. He was dressed in a black sport-coat with a basalt-tinted shirt; the top three buttons opened. Creasy's attire was complete with matching black pants and black shoes that absorbed all light, creating an illusion of Creasy's head hovering in thin air. Goosebumps pimpled Mike's body as he gaped at the re-fined Grimm Reaper.

"You have my dog," Creasy stated, picking imaginary grime from under his fingernails with his knife.

The sharp blade gunting as it trapped sparsely scattered moonlight. Mike tried not to shudder as dark bodies appeared from nowhere. As they circled the innocent, Mike flashed back to his dream:

Gang members cheered, circling my family like lions. The stand-off turned into a blood-bath as my father confronted the street thugs, defending my sister and mother as a courageous lion king protecting his pride from cackling hyenas. But despite his noblest of efforts, the king fell to his demise as the hyenas shred-ded my father to bits.

Mike's eyes darted from the dark faces to Creasy as he sized up his options, there weren't any. The warmth of the dog rubbed against his calf as the pit bull trembled under Mike. Creasy slinked towards them, eyeing Katelyn greedily.

"Who's your friend, Mike?" Creasy smiled.

Mike felt uneasy telling him about Katelyn.

"She's cute." Creasy lingered around Katelyn like a dog sniffing a bone. He touched her cheek when Mike spat, "Leave her alone!" Anger contorted his face into an irate stare. He watched Creasy's black eyes flicker, recognizing Mike's love for her.

"Ah! I see!" Creasy's smirk widened. "You two are…"

"Shut up!" Mike sneered as he punched Creasy's smiling teeth. Creasy cackled as two men lunged for Mike. Mike instinctively rammed one burly man in the nose. The bridge completely shattered as blood shot everywhere. But, the other one slapped Mike's head hard, and he stumbled to the asphalt. Blood trickled from Mike's throbbing head and his vision blurred as Katelyn was swept away by the shadow thugs. Mike tried to muscle his way to her but was too unsteady. Five cult members place a cloth over Katelyn's mouth, her emerald eyes rolled back as she was dragged away. Katelyn disappeared with the shadows.

"Pick him up," Creasy muttered as Mike watched the earth rotate upright and was dragged to his feet. "That's not going to fly, kid." Creasy mumbled, pinching the bridge of his nose to keep the blood from trickling down. "Why didn't you join us, Mike?" Mike knew Creasy was bitter about him turning the cult down. "I stuck my neck out for you."

"Your so-called 'hierarchy' is overseen by a bunch of psychopathic, mani-acs who get off by luring kids and making them do crazy shit. You really think they stand for justice?" Mike shot back.

"We have a purpose, Mike."

"Look at yourself, Alistair. Look at what you've become." Mike was almost sympathetic as he tried to talk sense to his friend, but as Mike looked into Alistair's eyes, he only saw a fog, spun from narcotics and brainwashing.

Creasy snorted the blood back into his nostrils as he calmly picked up his knife. Instinctively, Mike broke free, stomping on toes, then charged Creasy. But this time, Creasy was prepared. Suddenly, Mike felt the sharp blade as Creasy jammed the knife into his abdomen.

Staggering backwards, he traced the red spot that tarnished his Fighting Irish shirt. The green cotton and the blood seeping through Mike's burning wound converged into a dark navy color. Mike winced in pain. He did his best to keep pressure on the cut with his weak left arm as he slid his right hand in his pocket to dial Jim's number on his cell phone. As Creasy stared curiously, Mike caught sight of the morbid tattoo he remembered seeing years ago. When Creasy realized Mike's cell phone was sending out a call for help, he drew his knife and rammed it into Mike's chest. Mike felt a cold sting as the blade ripped through his pectoral muscle. He moaned as the pain spread through his chest like venom from a cobra.

"You know," Creasy said as he held the blade in Mike's chest, "I had a girlfriend once. Her name was Nina." Creasy smiled as residual blood dripped from his nose. "Nina was the most beautiful girl I'd ever seen. I'd do anything for her. But, she didn't love me..."

"I wonder why," Mike wheezed in pain. The continuous flow of blood from his chest drenched his hand. Mike clutched at the blade, fighting to dislodge it in Creasy's hand. He felt his life draining from his body while he struggled to maintain consciousness.

"She was hard to please," Creasy responded. "She couldn't get past the fact that I was different, like you. Trust me I'm doing you a favor," he said as he withdrew his knife, caked in viscous red. Blood dripped from the blade as Creasy wiped it on Mike's shirt.

Clinging to life by a thread, Mike's eyes rolled back into his head as darkness loomed over him. He could feel the coolness of the dark as he began to blackout. He envisioned his dead family gathering around his lifeless body, whispering the words, "Come home. Come home." Mike's spirit began ascending into the abyss. But, the hard squeal of tires dragged him back to awareness. Creasy quickly retreated to the shadows with his brutish crew.

Mike, feeble and wavering in and out of conscience, rolled onto his stomach trying to reach for the imaginary figure of Katelyn. Suddenly, he was being dragged out of the gritty alley toward help, his blood leaving a telltale trail.

Shit! Thought Creasy, *we lost the dog.* The injured canine vanished into the murky backstreet in the midst of the ensuing chaos. This annoyed Creasy. They had spent days searching for his prized fighter who became number one in the ranks after defeating the Champ. That dog earned its reputation of being the fiercest fighter in Boston and, if he continued to win, was going to make the cult wealthy. Then, Creasy would have been able to continue to aggressively expand the cult, establishing a circuit of members who lived in the states bordering Massachusetts and beyond. Yes, the cult would have spread like an infectious disease. It would have consolidated branches in all fifty states of America, if their money maker didn't limp off.

Creasy cursed Mike for his intrusion. Katelyn's kicking and screaming jostled Creasy from his thoughts, *well, at least we have the girl.* They swerved around the corner of Somerset, then barreled left down Ashburton Place. The driver peered at Creasy through the rear-view mirror and silently posed a question. Creasy gave Katelyn another sedative. She tried to bite him as he shoved the capsule down her throat. He thrust her chin upwards. "Swallow," Creasy ordered, pressing his palm against her chin so she wouldn't spit the capsule out. He watched the muscles in her throat strain as the pill slithered down her throat. Katelyn slowly went limp and her gorgeous green eyes closed. Creasy nodded to his driver. "Keep to the plan".

Jim's heart raced as he revved the V8 of his Trans Am Firebird down the weather-worn roads arriving just in time to see a black Mitsubishi peel away. Tires screeched as the car did a sharp one-eighty, peeling out of the alley. Jim jumped out of his car, gun drawn, emptying a round of ammunition into the fleeing car. There were five passengers: four men and one woman. As a sickening feeling sank, Jim realized Katelyn was taken. The slugs careened into the back fender. Cursing, he loaded a new clip, but it was too late. *What the hell happened? Where the hell is Mike?*

As Jim entered the gritty alley, he clutched his Glock 19, shining the strobe from the compact light clamped under the barrel in sweeping motions. The light could penetrate blinding darkness up to twenty-five feet, but the alley seemed to consume its effectiveness as Jim ventured deeper into the long passageway. He tried to ignore the ominous trepidation that haunted his thoughts since the moment he had awakened in an unusually silent house.

"Mike!" Jim tried to shoo away the creeping dread scratching at the walls of his mind. No answer. "Mike, answer me now!" Jim demanded as his fears escalated to desperation. Jim felt them grab him, shaking his nerves loose, as he heard a low growl. Cold sweat encased his palm as he threaded his finger snugly around the trigger. As he spun in the direction of the sneering, Jim stumbled on the graphic scene of Mike's body lying in a pool of blood. The injured pit bull crouched beside Mike's head; he bared his blood-stained teeth at Jim and gave a warning bark. *Just some random dog*, Jim assumed. Jim gingerly approached the pair trying to shoo away the dog. No luck, the animal remained at Mike's side, seemingly unimpressed by Jim's authority. It was then that Jim realized the dog was there protecting Mike.

"It's okay." Jim said, trying to calm the pit bull as he holstered the gun and shuffled closer. Jim grabbed Mike's legs and hauled him to his car while the dog followed on three legs. Unaware of the blood smears drying on his shirt, Jim tossed Mike into the backseat. He quickly checked Mike's pulse; it was weak, but it was there. Jim breathed a sigh of relief.

A ball of brindle scruff bounded into the car, nearly knocking Jim out of the way. Jim caught the edge of the opened door by two fingers, stumbling backwards. He regained his balance and saw the dog curled up in the back seat with Mike, dangling his swollen leg off the side of the seat.

"No! Out!" The dog, slightly foaming at the mouth, answered Jim's orders with a stubborn growl. Reluctantly, Jim surrendered to the pit bull's stand as he was more concerned with getting Mike medical help. Jim's heart was pounding, he felt fatigued and worried about the night's events. He knew the dawn would bring more of an opportunity to better analyze the situation and to find those bastards who had Katelyn. He didn't care if he had to tear Boston apart building by building. He was going to get his daughter back. He knew Mike would be there with him, searching the city with the same ferocity as Jim.

Turning back to the four-legged beast guarding Mike, Jim made a mental note to drop the dog at a veterinarian after rushing Mike to the hospital. The Trans Am tore out of the alleyway. In his rear-view mirror, Jim watched the pit bull lap up Mike's blood pooling in the backseat. He had to hurry.

Lead-footing the accelerator, Jim darted along the barren backstreets, his heart in his throat. The situation finally crystalizing in his mind; his adopted son lay in his own blood and his daughter was God-knows-where. Jim's nerves rattled as he punched 9-1-1 into his mobile phone and reported his daughter missing. Jim's green eyes swelled with tears as he raced toward Massachusetts General Hospital.

Mike awoke in a hospital bed, attached to a monitor and an IV, pumping fluids through his veins. He squinted at the glaring aura of light gleaming above him. He followed a pair of scrubs walking across the room checking his vital signs.

"Mike? Can you hear me? How do you feel?" Jim's voice funneled through a dreamlike channel, circulating in grainy waves around Mike's head. His blurry vision refocused to a crystal-clear mural of white walls that encircled the room. *I'm in the hospital*, Mike recognized after studying his surroundings. Jim was standing at the foot of the bed in a denim button-down shirt and jeans.

Mike's head throbbed. He reached to delicately massage his forehead. He shuttered as a needle of pain threaded his chest.

"Fuck!" he mumbled as he felt the lace of stitches. The knife wound burned with every breath. Mike lifted his hospital gown to find 15 stitches embroidered across his shaved chest.

"You're in the hospital and lucky to be alive," Jim said.

"I know," Mike grumbled, frustrated about the predicament he had fallen into, dragging Katelyn along for the perilous ride. "I remember everything." He swallowed hard. His scratchy throat felt as arid as an Arabian desert. Mike surmised the trach tube had a part in that. He stared at Jim, dreading to ask about Katelyn. The night began so perfectly. It felt so right. Now, Mike regretted every bit of it, except for kissing Katelyn. He still felt her tenderness padlocked in his heart forever. "I know who did it," Mike said.

Mike outlined the night's events to Jim, every excruciating detail, except the kiss, of course. A heavy burden of guilt cemented itself deeply in his heart. Now that his world had been shattered by Creasy, Mike cringed when Katelyn's vibrant green eyes crossed his mind.

Jim jotted notes on a small notepad as he listened intently. Mike explained how he and Katelyn found the injured pit bull, he described their encounter with Creasy, and how the twisted man had threatened their lives and fled with Katelyn. It was like peeling an onion. The further Mike revealed the rotten details, the worse it stunk. Mike watched as Jim's heavy heart sank lower and lower.

Ending the painful narrative, Mike watched intently, allowing Jim time to digest the facts. He saw the emotional pain etched on Jim's face. Staring into Jim's green eyes, Mike saw a hint of Katelyn looking back. His lips suddenly scorched with her sweet taste. He stored the taste of the kiss in his heart as a memento for his own private investigation. Mike watched Jim's face grow beat-red with anger.

"You know this Alistair Creasy?"

"Yes. He was my friend from high school," Mike said.

"What is he like?" Jim asked.

"Not the kind of guy to be taken lightly." Mike shook his head, feeling his mind refocus. "He was into cult shit. Dark magic shit. He might have been a member of one. He has this weird tattoo on his neck." Mike re-imagined the ominous tattoo, tracing the spot behind his own ear. He shuddered.

"Do you have a picture of Creasy?" Jim asked.

"No," Mike replied. He realized that he had no evidence of their friendship other than intangible memories. But then, he remembered his high school year book. Surely, it contained a snapshot of Creasy. "But, Creasy's picture is in my yearbook."

Mike gazed at the four pasty hospital walls that stared back bleakly. He had always suffered from a phobia of hospitals. Mike ripped the nasal cannula tube from his face and got dressed when a nurse walked in.

"All better." Mike smiled at her, as he left with Jim. "Gotta check on my dog," he said, surprising himself.

Gomez awoke from a long state of unconsciousness in the same hospital. His mind was a nauseating fog, and he could feel the heroin had drained from his system, abandoning his body as it dwindled to ash. Gomez squinted up at the florescent light, which diffused in dome-like auras that clouded his weary head. The socket of his left shoulder insistently moaned in stiffness as his arm dangled above his head. Gomez tried to readjust when the rigid, cold metal grip of handcuffs ripped into his wrist like a hangman's noose.

"Good morning," A north-Boston voice greeted Gomez.

Befuddled at first, Gomez peered at the lean figure standing next to the hospital bed.

"I'm Detective Jim Miller from the Boston Police Department." The man stepped into the light showing his police shield to Gomez. Then, Gomez looked away as he remembered the dog fight and how it went dreadfully awry.

"I need to ask you a couple of questions, Mr. Gomez," Detective Miller pulled up a chair and began. Gomez had two options; reject the whole probing process or comply, with a possible reduced sentence and the satisfaction of sinking Creasy's whole enterprise, while saving his own daughter from Creasy's grip. The choice was obvious.

Mike stared at the picture of Creasy's evil complexion, with vexing hatred boiling in his stomach and his farewell kiss to Katelyn swirling in his memory. The chaotic rush of feelings burned his head, as the lighting in the narrow cube twinkled above him. They had uploaded the photo to Jim's computer. Jim then posted it to BPD's police database, typing in Creasy's last name, forename, nationality, gender, and age. In addition, the online database asked for Creasy's eye color and hair color.

Mike flipped open his cell phone, checking the time. He squinted into the light, as crippling pain settled right above his eyes. The day broke into early afternoon. He had to convene with veterinarian Dr. Bates within the hour to discuss the dog's prognosis. Mike dreaded the fact that mending the pit bull's broken leg would whack almost his entire savings, but his moral compass ultimately decided his course of action.

There was no doubt he had been abused. The dog had suffered multiple scars from other dogs probably twice his size, according to the vet's analysis.

Mike watched Dr. Bates examine the pit bull. She showed Mike the x-rays, indicating the dog's broken femur was healing with help from an implanted plate and screws. "On a person, the fracture would be in your thigh bone," she explained.

"What's his name?" Dr. Bates explained they needed more information to complete the dog's record. Mike pondered for a moment, trying to think of a name. He was distracted by a long-ago memory when Katelyn told him her favorite recording artists were The Beatles, especially Ringo Star. "Ringo," Mike uttered, with a smile in his heart.

He listened to the conversation from the safety of his discreet Mitsubishi, stationed at the northeast corner of the parking deck. Tinted windows cloaked the passenger in a secure blanket as he communicated with his hospital contact. Creasy gained valuable information. The nurse, one of his cult members, planted a bug in Gomez's room. Now, Creasy could hear the unabridged version of Detective Jim Miller's interrogation.

Creasy adjusted his earpiece, fine-tuning it to hone in on their quiet mumbles. His tattoo burned with anguish when Gomez mentioned the cult, making him sweat under his collar. He knew this would not sit well with the elders.

"Creasy works with a league of shadows," Gomez said.

"What do you mean?" the detective pried.

Creasy breathed slowly and deliberately in the still of the night. He mastered the art of concealment, veiling himself behind imaginary shaded curtains as all great predators do. He listened intently.

"I don't know who they are, but I was helping to put on fights for them. I used to sell Creasy heroin, until he got me arrested. After that, I decided to hang low. Then, he came back. He wanted money. They are holding my daughter as leverage," Gomez said.

"Who's 'they'?" Jim asked.

"I told you, I don't know," Gomez stuttered.

"What does your daughter look like?" the cop sighed. His voice seemed to take on a softer texture. Detective Miller, Creasy noted, apparently shared Gomez's pain. *It keeps getting juicier*, thought Creasy as his eyes lit up and a nefarious grin spread from ear to ear.

"Short. Black hair. Beautiful," Gomez said.

"How tall?" Detective Miller continued after a brief pause. There was hurt in Miller's hardy, North Boston accent. Creasy knew he had heard a similar accent from… Creasy felt his jaws throb as he covered his mouth and cackled.

Katelyn Miller.

Creasy returned to his lair where he kept hostages. He pranced down the halls and hopped over the floorboards under which Katelyn Miller was hidden; sedated, bound, and gagged. Creasy grinned at his computer screen as he hatched an idea: he would hack Miller's police account where he'd have access to convicted felons for recruit into the cult. He could then tap into a network of prisons and enlist a point man who would actively engage potential members to stage a prison break. Within a few keystrokes, he was in South Bay House of Correction, tapping into the roster of prisoners. After identifying his point man, he began implementing his whirlwind idea. With the ability to tap into the prison's surveillance cameras, he could watch the prison break unfold. The surveillance footage showed rows of cell doors closed – for now. Soon enough he would relish his victory. *This is damn good.* Creasy praised himself as he rolled a well-deserved joint. As he smoothed out the creases in the thin shell, he thought about how much wilier he was than the police. The elders would certainly be proud, Creasy mused as he lit the cigarette, wrapping his lips around the smooth piece of wheat.

He checked his watch. He needed to be at the fighting arena in an hour to greet customers and take bets. He snubbed the joint after one last, deep drag. There was just a couple of loose ends to tie up; Hernando Gomez and Mike Craven.

Mike stared into Katelyn's green eyes. Her angelic grin tickled his heart. They danced in the spotlight of a bright, golden sun. He could feel packed grains of sand under his feet as he twirled her about. She loved the beach. They had taken occasional trips to the shore where they could enjoy mini escapes from the day-to-day, chore-filled life. They slowly stopped, as Mike was drawn in by Katelyn's strikingly beautiful eyes. He kissed her as the rays of the golden sun burned his cheek.

Mike opened his eyes to be disappointed by the four walls of the animal hospital's lobby. The four plain walls looked as depressed and as sleep-deprived as he was. As he lifted his head from the rough plaster, Jim walked in. Mike scraped crusty gunk from the corners of his eyes. Jim plopped into the seat next to him and said, "You were right about Creasy."

"And you doubted me?" Mike was unimpressed by Jim's revelation.

"There's a drug dealer in the same hospital you were in and he can confirm the existence of the cult. I checked with BPD undercover and the FBI field agent, they have the cult under surveillance."

This information jostled Mike from his daydream state of mind. "You're telling me they know?!"

"Law enforcement wants to infiltrate the cult like they did the Irish mob. Get inside their organization and get a step ahead of their game plan." Mike paused, feeling a twinge of curiosity tickle his mind.

"They in yet?" Mike queried.

"Not sure, they wouldn't confirm that info," Jim responded.

It occurred to Mike that he could be the law's infiltrator. *Why not? I've been approached before, I could do this. I could help. I could get Katelyn out. I could turn evidence that would bury Creasy, The Mentor and all the scumbags associated with them. What are the chances?*

"We need to focus on exposing the cult instead of trying to book Creasy on abduction and drug charges." Mike knew his idea was far-fetched and the task would be tough, but he was willing to put himself out there for Katelyn. Nervously, he shared his concept with Jim.

Astonished, Jim didn't respond in the supportive way Mike thought he would. "Are you fucking nuts?!" Jim exploded. It was so outrageous, it just might work. They set up a meeting with BPD undercover and the FBI.

Jim led the way as he and Mike walked through the police station. They met with Jim's captain and FBI agents sent to help Boston's finest come up with a strategy to eliminate the threat of the cult. The FBI field agent quarterbacking the situation appeared skeptical when Mike and Jim met with him, along with Jim's captain. As they sat in the captain's office, Mike noticed the slightly puzzled looks on their faces. They exchanged brief introductions before getting to business; Special Agents Hardy and Goldman.

For the majority of the meeting, Jim allowed Mike to fill everyone in on Creasy and the cult since he knew the most. Listening intently, Hardy and Goldman allowed Mike to finish uninterrupted. When Mike was done, Hardy and Goldman shot each other incredulous glances.

"This is real. I've got the scars to prove it." Mike tapped the table in annoyance.

"We understand," said Hardy. "It's just we've never heard first-hand accounts."

"Look," Jim stepped in. "We have the facts, we need hard evidence. Mike got stabbed before these assholes took my daughter. At the very least, we can book them on attempted murder and abduction."

"Okay. So, what do you propose?" Goldman asked. Mike jumped in, "Let me be your informant. I know how to handle these guys. I can get the evidence you need and, more important, I can save Detective Miller's daughter but we gotta move fast."

Creasy grinned devilishly at Massachusetts General Hospital's emergency escape plan, as he studied the escape route for the third level, on which Gomez's room would render him a dead man, amongst the chaos. He motioned for two medics, who were his inside men, and instructed them to lock the door. McFarlane and Ines nodded, complying. "Make sure you set the alarm first. You guys gotta make a beeline for Gomez and get everyone else evacuated. But, there needs to be other casualties so it looks like an accident."

Of course," the pair acknowledged, then, dismissed by Creasy, they headed toward the pale landmark that grazed Boston's skyline.

For a brief moment, Creasy nostalgically stared at the gallant building which would infamously commemorate the turning point for his cult. *And so it begins*, Creasy mused. The explosion lit up Boston's stark midnight sky like a candle on a birthday cake, the cult's first birthday cake. Glass shattered from windows that overlooked the hospital's urban backyard, flames from the inferno ascended into the sky forming a black canopy of smoke. Creasy silently saluted his departed cult brethren, McFarlane and Ines, who sacrificed their lives. The black Mitsubishi slowly pulled away, merging seamlessly into the traffic on Cambridge Street. Adrenaline pumped steadily through his veins, as he heard distant sirens blaring.

Mike and Jim cruised into Roxbury in a dark-colored, undercover Crowne Vic. The town's inception was conceived by the British and was the home of English, Irish, and German immigrants, threading a century of diverse European bloodlines. Mike recollected learning about a massive migration of African Americans that dominated the region even in present day. The setting sun crept low on the horizon now, and, as it peeped through sparse trees and alleyways, its beacons of light gave background illumination to Roxbury's neighborhoods.

As they ventured further into conclaves of drug dealers and addicts, old ghosts from the past visited Mike. Years earlier, a dozen pairs of glassy eyes would stare at Mike as he passed these residences, returning to his Southie home from school. A blade of uncertainty sliced through Mike as he peered through the windshield of Jim's Crowne Vic.

As they steered onto Veterans of Wars Parkway, Mike felt a throb of irony pulse through him. The name was a lofty title for such a miserable, depressed landscape. Over-grown lawns guarded the border of the slowly-withering tenements, as hordes of termites ate away at wooden clapboard siding. Barking canines snarled, as the Crowne Vic rolled past, arousing their masters' attention. A bald man ambled onto his small porch grasping an old M-1 rifle. The man's penetrating stare scrutinized the unmarked cruiser as Jim parked across Lot 1469 and killed the engine.

"This is it," Jim whispered as Mike hesitantly left the safety of the cruiser. Outside, goose bumps pricked up on the back of his neck as a familiar sense of danger roused his senses. Mike followed Jim as they strode toward the front door, surveying the dilapidated cottage. Gashes in the tenement's exterior exposed its pink insulation, like shredded human flesh. Jim took out tools to effortlessly pick the lock.

Inside, Gomez's residence was filled with dust and grime. The place seemed forlorn, waiting in the dark for its master to return. There was a slight chill in the house, and the odor of mildew dangled in the air. They swept the house for a hint that could help explain the cult's incentive for abducting Gomez's daughter, other than the obvious, to gain Gomez's cooperation. They combed through the front part of the house without luck, then headed to the back.

The rear of the house was bleaker then the front. Scent of stale narcotics wafted through the entire shack, gagging Mike. Even though it was the same stench Mike had lived with for a little over a decade, his immunity toward the odor had diminished considerably on his hiatus away from the smog, living with his adopted family.

Covering his mouth and nose, Mike followed Jim into a small kitchen area, which was empty aside from a refrigerator, a gas stove, and a cluster of chairs spread apart in disarray. To their right loomed a dark hall of closed doors. They meandered around scattered roaches, discarded cardboard boxes, rolls of masking tape, and empty cigarette packets, to the first door on the left.

"You check that room," Jim said, pointing to the door. "I'll check the others." Still holding his breath, Mike nodded, taking his hand away from his nose and mouth as he turned the doorknob. He could hear Jim's feet stomping on the creaky floor. Four bubble-gum pink walls, wallpapered with faded posters of wild ponies screamed "girl's room" at Mike as he stepped into the brightness. A single bed was the centerpiece of the room. It was in pristine condition, like the rest of the bedroom. There was a small desk, flush against the wall to Mike's left, flooded with papers. Mike began rummaging through the pile, anxious to uncover a connection that could clue him in on Creasy's heinous plans.

On the desk, a pink sticky note had a name and a phone number. Mike picked up the memo and showed Jim.

"I know this guy." Jim said. "He's a probation officer. I'm gonna call him. Keep looking."

Jim fished out his phone as he exited the room. Moments later, Jim returned with news. "Gomez's probation officer said Leonza had called, wanting to turn her dad in. He said that was the last time he spoke with her." Before Mike could respond, Jim's phone rang.

"Yeah?" Jim answered. Jim's face took on a look of bewilderment and irritation. "Well, did they ID him?" Jim asked angrily. Following Jim's blunt inquiry was a stretched sigh, his face appearing flustered. The room suddenly became dimmer and colder. "I'm at Gomez's residence right now. I'll be there," Jim said as he snapped the silver phone shut and shoved it into his pocket.

"Gomez is dead," Jim uttered in a cold, mechanical tone.

Mass General had been partially annihilated. Flames of orange and red still flickered atop the charred rubble, as Jim's Crowne Vic pulled up behind some black and white cruisers, their flashing lights casting the crime scene in pulsating red and blue hues. As the Vic mounted the curb, Jim told Mike to remain in the car while he met with a police officer.

"It looks like the bomb was placed in a corner of the third level. Room 123," Officer Ramirez told Jim.

"Of course. They ID Gomez?" Jim asked.

"Yes. The nursing staff did."

This had Creasy's name stamped all over it. Jim stepped over a mound of blackened rubble toward BPD's coroner, Bob Harlem. Besides Gomez's burned corpse, Harlem stooped over two other bodies. Gomez's hospital gown had been almost entirely decimated, exposing third-degree burns on Gomez's body. Jim smelled the corpse's burned flesh as he saw Gomez's face covered in soot. Jim felt melancholy, as he looked upon the corpse of the man he spoke to just hours before.

Mike silently brooded in the passenger seat of the Crowne Vic, watching a few snippets of fire lap at the hospital remains. Mike used to think Creasy's dark side was just a phase that he would eventually grow out of. But now, as Mike watched half-scorched bodies being zipped up in body-bags and survivors lifted into ambulances, it was apparent to him that Creasy truly knew no boundaries. He was in awe that one man was the cause all of this destruction. His mind throbbed with disgust and he felt the scar imprinted on his chest burn. He needed to end it.

Mike flipped his cellphone open and scrolled through his contacts. Mike's heart pounded in his chest as he planned to offer Creasy a deal he knew Creasy would find too lucrative to pass up. He selected Creasy's number and pressed the call button on the phone's keypad. The pain in Mike's chest faded as he took on a cold, emotionless persona waiting for Creasy's Southie whine to answer. Mike heard only one ring before Creasy's nasally voice answered, "Yeah?"

"Creasy. I have a proposition." Mike spoke through clenched teeth as he offered a deal to the psychopath. "Let's hear it," Creasy skeptically replied as a slight wheeze broke the phone's background static. Mike closed his eyes and visualized Creasy sitting in the dark, enjoying his cigarette. He could hear the unmistakable rasp of a smoker in Creasy's voice. Mike heard Creasy turn away from the phone and begin to cough. As the coughing continued, Mike wondered how long Creasy had been a smoker. Up until now, Mike hadn't paid much attention to Creasy's sporadic coughing jigs. "We trade. I pledge loyalty to the cult, giving you access to police intel which you need to grow your membership and avoid detection, and you let Katelyn go."

"Cops put you up to this? You think I'm stupid?" Creasy asked incredulously.

"No. My deal, my deal alone." Mike answered.

"Why?" Creasy shot back.

"It's because of me that you have Katelyn. She's no good to you. Her dad won't turn, he's too good a cop. I'm not. I'll give you whatever you want." Mike concluded with resolve. He hoped his act was convincing.

Creasy thought long and hard. How could he trust Mike? Mike turned him down once before. How convenient that he wants to join now. As Creasy negotiated the whirlwind of questions swirling in his head, Mike interrupted. "One more thing. You have Gomez's daughter, Leonza. Let her go too. I've got Gomez's probation officer's ear. I can discredit anything Leonza says. And ..... I've got your prize fighting dog." Mike said, thinking this would make his offer even sweeter.

"Do we have a deal or not?" Mike asked again, becoming frustrated with Creasy's games. Mike's stomach seized into a knot as the burning returned to his scar. Mike cupped his left hand over the wound where the pain congregated like an angry mob, spearing Mike's gut with cutting pitchforks. He did not speak until the blade of pain dissolved. Creasy answered, "Yes."

He took a deep breath, relieved from the pain and hung up. Lifting his shirt, Mike traced the sutures in the wound, making sure none had popped. He counted the stitches as he gently traced the group of laces with his finger. All of them were still intact. Mike wondered if the discomfort was from the wound or did it actually hurt to say he would make a pact with Creasy?

Mike stepped out of the car to tell Jim about the deal he made when his phone received a text message from Creasy. "Come alone," it read. The keys were in the ignition. Mike knew this was a delicate situation that could easily go awry if he didn't follow Creasy's exact demands. The lives of two women hung in the balance. One wrong decision could end either, maybe both, lives. Mike obeyed Creasy's orders like a dog eager to please his master.

Lynn, dubbed "the city of sin" because of its reputation for criminal activity, was Mike's destination per Creasy's text messages. Wild thoughts topped Mike's mind, thoughts of Creasy tormenting Katelyn, which stirred conflicting feelings; but, Creasy called the shots now, and he wanted a 'safe' meeting location. Before getting out of the car, Mike remembered Jim had an extra gun locked in the glove box. He quietly thanked Jim.

Mike found himself on the corner of Rogers Avenue clutching the black grip of a loaded Smith & Wesson revolver, surveying the once quaint New England neighborhood. He pondered why Creasy chose this location to meet. Of course, its reputation of making people insane, probably appealed to the depraved cult member. *THE* cult. There must be a small city in which the cult lays low and off of the Boston police's radar. Mike knew of a quaint, sparsely-populated island off the coast of Lynn, named Nahant. *Perfect for keeping a cult under wraps*, Mike thought.

The street grew dark as dense clouds gathered overhead, wrapping their menacing fingers around the moon's glimmering face, smothering it. Mike stood, waiting in solid darkness, alone on the vacant stretch of the dead city's floor. Only a few lone cars sped down the street for a short dash of seconds. The squeal of tires peeling away left him with a ghost of loneliness, breathing cold tingles down his spine, leaving him in a valley of nothingness.

Mike squeezed the hidden pistol's grip, testing his hold, summoning his courage. Nervous sweat seeped from his palm, trickling down the butt of the weapon. With trembling hands, Mike spun the barrel around to confirm each slot of the barrel was packed with a bullet. The moon burst through the maze of ashen clouds, pouring a haze of pale light upon Mike's face as his heart raced.

Flanagan rode in the passenger seat of the Lincoln with a thirst for resurrection. He clutched his Beretta, brooding about how Creasy single-handedly turned his outfit against him. He was baffled by how quickly the desertion spread throughout the Irish mob. They hopped on Creasy's bandwagon within moments of his appearance. Not surrendering and determined to win back his crew, Flanagan implemented his old-fashion spy work. He had immediately positioned his few remaining loyal soldiers to spy on Creasy with the intent of re-establishing his dominance as the alpha-dog. His men witnessed Creasy providing the ex-mobsters with easy access to drugs and leading them in rituals. Flanagan himself staked out the "mob-turned-cult" at Saint Bridge. He recorded them in a "spiritual enlightenment". Flanagan could not believe what he saw.

Flanagan found Creasy repulsive. Creasy was demoralizing the former mobsters, turning them into robotic terrorists. In Flanagan's opinion, Creasy's criminal intent would lead to the Irish mob's demise. Flanagan could not let that happen. And so, there he was, wading in the dark, traveling the road to retribution in Lynn; Lynn the city of sin. Flanagan and his loyal posse drove through the dark streets, where a tipster claimed to have spotted Creasy. Cruising by densely constructed buildings, a flash of some figure caught his eye. Flanagan ordered the driver to slow down as they cruised the dimly lit side street. Flanagan recognized a skinny figure in the night, loitering anxiously on the side of the road, clinging to a poorly hidden revolver.

The lean, young man paid no attention to Flanagan's black Lincoln. He seemed to be ruminating intensely while nervously fidgeting in place. As the moon peered out from behind ominous clouds, Flanagan recognized Mike Craven. Flanagan paused, curiously studying Mike. The young man seemed to be cast under a dangerous spell of anger.

The Lincoln pulled over to nestle inconspicuously in the darkness among a trio of cars already parked in the quiet backstreet, cornered by buildings of brick, some with awnings which made the night seem even darker. Abruptly, the hairs on Flanagan's neck stood on end, as a jet-black Mitsubishi sedan screeched to the curb. Smoke waivered off the burned rubber as a group of men in black suits snatched Mike and wrestled him into the trunk.

"Go!" Flanagan urged his driver as the Mitsubishi sped off. He felt something for the kid. He didn't know what. It might have been old-age remorse for his past violent history with the Craven clan. Flanagan also knew from his intel that Mike was up to something. Recognizing Creasy's Mitsubishi, Flanagan wasn't going to let this opportunity escape him.

Darkness suffocated Mike. The stuffy trunk reeked of mold and, even though the oxygen level in the cramped space was high, he could hear his own breathing quicken. Mike took his cell phone from his pocket and called Jim, knowing that Jim would have it traced, pin-pointing Mike's location. As the car swerved to the right and left, Mike was slammed against the interior of the trunk. He tried covering his head with his hands until his fingers were brutally crunched between his head and the side of the trunk.

The revolver was holstered in the waistband of Mike's jeans. He didn't think any of his captors had suspected that he was armed. The Mitsubishi suddenly slowed to an idle crawl, gently rocking over bumps. Mike heard the engine rev when the car came to a halt. The engine died, and Mike heard feet stomping pavement as doors were slammed shut. Then, muffled chatting took place as Mike held his breath, concentrating on the dialog. Katelyn was the topic of the muffled, gruff voices.

"Bring her into the catacombs," Creasy's nasally voice barked. Hurried footsteps clamored, obeying the mandate subpoenaed by Creasy. The dragging of feet painted the picture of Creasy's cultic brethren hauling Katelyn away. Mike grabbed his Smith & Wesson revolver as a plan brewed in his mind. His pulse quickened as he heard footsteps sloshing through gravel, coming closer to the trunk. Mike silently clicked back the hammer, inching the barrel of the revolver close to the narrow fissure where the door and the rest of the trunk locked. Mike's pounding heart rocketed into his throat as the trunk finally popped open.

"Don't move!" Mike growled bestially as he clutched Creasy's arm, jamming the revolver in Creasy's ribs. He saw the surprised reactions of Creasy's thugs, some immediately aiming their pistols at his head, while others hesitated to pull their weapons. Knowing that, as their leader, Creasy had the upper hand, Mike gouged his Smith & Wesson deeper into Creasy's ribs.

"Tell your men to drop their guns, or else I shoot," Mike muttered to Creasy as he slowly wound his finger around the trigger. "Drop the guns," Creasy hollered to the army of men in black—their necks engraved with the same morbid tattoo as Creasy's. Mike's hand began to tremble from the adrenaline rush.

Slowly, every single one lowered their weapons. Mike gingerly climbed out of the trunk while maintaining his hold on Creasy. He kept Creasy at point-blank range to ensure none of the cult members would try anything funny. Mike knew he must maintain control of the situation and that he was walking a tightrope to keep the upper hand.

"Where is Katelyn?" Mike hissed to Creasy. "I want to see her. Then we settle this, just you and me."

"Of course," Creasy jeered back, chuckling in the back of his throat. "Ma-no-a-mano," Creasy muttered and began to shuffle toward the rustic stone entrance of the catacombs. "Stand down, brethren," Creasy's nasally voice resonated off the ancient masonry as Mike shoved him into the dark, gloomy entrance of the catacombs.

The dingy underground route was even more dismal than its shabby external frame. No matter the strength of rays, no light could penetrate its black gloom. Fear tormented all of Mike's senses as he followed Creasy, maintaining his hold on the vile tyrant, descending into the earth through the stone tunnel. The hairs on the back of his neck quivered in fear, as shadows swallowed the two. He chased his fears away, by reminding himself that Katelyn waited at the end of the murky tunnel to be saved. Then, he became lost in the comforting memory of her kiss.

"I'm not surprised, you know. Didn't really think you had the balls to join." Creasy casually commented. "Keep walking!" Mike snapped. The air was becoming thin and cool. The echo of their feet treading the slanting stone floor carried further into the dark corridor. The cave's endless meandering gave Mike the impression that Creasy was leading him on a wild goose chase. Just then, he heard moans of a young woman. Mike speared Creasy with the revolver, urging him to pick up the pace.

As they approached, Mike saw a young woman bound to a chair with a thick band of duct-tape suctioned to her mouth. Her complexion was that of a rich walnut. Her striking eyes were like hazelnuts. Her face was battered and bruised, no doubt that the young woman had been beaten. Blood decorated her swollen face like war paint. Her eyes rolled back into her skull from the devastating trauma she must have endured. It was Leonza.

A ghostly shadow appeared, abruptly slamming Mike against the wall. The brute force of the agonizing body shot pinned him against the cave's jagged interior. His gun fired, sending bullets into the darkness. The jolt freed Creasy, and he disappeared into another tunnel, venturing further into the catacombs. The thug wrestled with Mike as Mike tenaciously held onto his weapon. Finally breaking free, Mike quickly took aim and shot the thug in the head. His blood sprayed the catacombs as Mike rushed to Leonza. Her head slumped down, and she was as still as a corpse. He pressed two fingers on her neck for a pulse. Nothing. Looking closer, he saw one of the stray bullets lodged in her chest. "Shit!"

A crushing blow from behind sent Mike to his knees; a second, dropped him on the rugged stone floor. A droplet of viscous sap rolled down his cold face and then dribbled onto his knuckle. Before a shade of unconsciousness swallowed him whole, Mike noticed the drop of blood on his knuckle.

Surrounded by the night, Flanagan could barely see the catacombs that lay before him. He had parked his Lincoln twenty yards away from the catacombs, behind some dense foliage and left the black car in hiding. Before leaving the town car, Flanagan injected his Beretta with a new magazine, betting he would go through every single round.

He led a posse of four into the catacombs. Each man concealed a fully-loaded gun. Each magazine contained twelve rounds, and every one needed to count. Flanagan switched the Beretta's compact light on as they crept toward the catacombs. As he was the first of his posse to enter the sloping corridor, Flanagan aimed the powerful strobe of light into the cave's mouth. But the thick fog of blackness gulped down the light's powerful ray. Flanagan began to sweat, entering the dank atmosphere of the desecrated burial site. He loosened his tie and unbuttoned his collar, as he felt strangled by the white button-down piece of his thirty-year-old pin-striped Armani suit. Flanagan left his black wool Fedora back in his Lincoln, knowing that it would be tucked safely away from the gunfire that would most likely occur within the catacombs.

As they ventured deeper into the underground bunker, Flanagan cringed as he heard the buzzing echo of Creasy's Southie accent. He shined the beam of the compact light upon the rocky path, cautiously planting his feet, as he shuffled along the steep-sloping path. He swept the light across the cave's width when something nestled in a rut within the bedrock caught the lights, Flanagan signaled for his posse to remain silent as Creasy's voice boomed through the tunnel.

"Wakey, wakey, Mikey..." The distant voice of Creasy cooed. A blurry face inches away from the tip of Mike's nose focused into the grinning Irish-Italian mug-shot of Alistair Creasy.

"Ah! He's coming around," Creasy said, peering at Mike. He shined a pen-light in Mike's eyes. Mike squinted as the small strobe of light waved unsteadi-ly over his eyes. Dried blood crusted the side of his face. A gathering of black-hooded cult members surrounded him. He squinted as his eyes tried refocusing in the swirling maelstrom of darkness.

Mike was slouched backwards against the hard metal back of a chair and his hands were strewn together around the rigid backrest. It deeply gouged his shoulder, tingling his nerves with tranquilizing numbness. Propping himself upright against the uncomfortable backrest, the stitch of mild discomfort flushed down his right arm as the ominous echo of deliberate footsteps cap-tured his full attention. Goosebumps rose from Mike's clammy skin.

Not uttering a word, Creasy walked six long, reverberating strides into the pitch-black abyss looming over his shoulder. Mike heard feminine groans as Creasy pulled Katelyn from the veil of opaque shadows. A bullet of sadness grazed Mike's heart as he stared at the hostage.

"You have me, Creasy. Now, let Katelyn go," Mike ordered as he watched Creasy standing beside Katelyn with his switch blade in hand. Slicing through the darkness with over-bearing authority, the switch blade parted the circle around Mike, allowing him to watch its master taunt Katelyn. Mike withheld from shouting at Creasy as his face burned with frustration. He felt helpless, tied to his chair with goons surrounding him who were loyal dogs of Creasy. Mike bet none of them would budge unless Creasy commanded them to do so.

"We still need her for your 'initiation,'" Creasy said as he stood behind Kate-lyn with the blade of his knife gently resting on her throat. Mike needed to stall long enough to form a plan.

"Why?" Mike frowned.

"Because you're going to trade her in exchange for my dog," Creasy snick-ered.

"I don't have him," Mike shrugged, stalling. "I need to get him first."

"No worries, we've already sent word to Miller. He brings the dog, he gets his daughter." Creasy cackled, quite pleased with himself.

Meanwhile, shrouded in darkness and quiet as mice, Flanagan and his posse began forming their own plan.

Jim turned down the gravel road, scared for Katelyn and Mike's lives. The Crowne Vic stumbled over the loose gravel that pelted the car's undercarriage like bullets. He parked the car off to the side of the road and explored the rest of the path on foot, his footsteps quickening as he continued further down the long gravel path. The tactical light that guided his way to the catacombs combed the dark path in a sweeping motion. Beads of sweat ran down Jim's large forehead as he saw the entrance of a sub-terrain passageway looming in the distance. Jim slowed his gait as he neared the ominous portal, studying it. Sweat built under his arms and he smelled his own body odor. Jim was suddenly blasted by cool air as he lingered near the entrance of the catacombs.

Jim suddenly lost his footing and grappled for something to hold onto finding a small cavity to grasp. As he hoisted himself up, he peered into the catacomb where he caught a glimpse of its walls. Nausea spiraled through Jim, as he realized the walls were composed of decayed skulls. Jim could feel the pupils of ghosts watch him descend through the earth. Collecting himself, Jim looked down at the slanting terrain and mapped out a path that was somewhat leveled and tightroped the thin walkway. It snaked through a maze of the deceased as it lowered Jim further into the catacombs. Jim reached the bottom where the dark was thickest and the air was the coolest. He knew he was being watched. He could sense it.

A shade passed by. Jim flipped the safety off, aiming the Glock in its direction.

He was about to call out when a hand clamped over his mouth. The meaty hand gently turned Jim around and held a finger to a pair of lips. "Sshh…" Flintlock Flanagan mouthed. Behind Flanagan, his posse crouched, waiting for further instructions. The group was small. Five men total. Jim and Flanagan used gestures to communicate. Jim pointed to the group, indicating he wanted them to hang back and then he signaled that he and Flanagan should check out the situation. Flanagan frowned and started whispering.

"There's a small army down there. A shitload of firepower. One wrong move and we're done. If we go down there, we should have at least two of my men for backup."

"Okay." Jim agreed, "But, nobody does anything unless I say. Got it?" Jim asserted, sending the message that he was in charged. "Sure." Flanagan said with a smug grin. "You're the boss."

A loose flake of stone fumbled down a steep slope off to the far right corner, making Creasy and company flinch. Mike's heart pulsated with excitement as he sensed the presence of help. In the corner of his eye, Mike briefly saw an outline and recognized the dark figure now hidden, crouching behind a large mural of skulls. It was Jim. For a split-second, Jim's compact light attached to his Glock reflected off his glasses and shined under his gray mustache. Scrambling footsteps echoed in the dank cave as Creasy immediately reeled Katelyn back into the shadows while several pistols were shoved into Mike's face. His heart sank as Katelyn screeched and was dragged back into the dark. Behind one of the glaring barrels inches away from his nose, Mike could see the black handle of his revolver jutting from the large thug's waistband. The black grip of the Smith & Wesson was barely reachable.

The thug clicked back the hammer of his pistol, grinning at Mike fiendishly, unveiling a set of rotten teeth. The thug was so close to Mike, that Mike could feel the warmth of his rancid breath crawl down his green, Fighting Irish t-shirt. He didn't want to die like this. Mike closed his eyes and pictured himself lounging on a beach with Katelyn. A resonating bang pierced his daydream. His heart skipped a beat. Mike opened his eyes to see a gaping wound in the thug's chest. Blood drained from the bullet wound as the thug collapsed, dead. The other cult brethren spun toward a large boulder and began a deafening volley of shots.

Throwing himself on the cold, moist floor, Mike crawled on his stomach, through the thug's pooling blood to retrieve his revolver. The black handle, now coated in the thug's blood, suctioned to Mike's palm, as he began shooting adjoining clusters of thugs that aimed their pistols at Jim. He realized his aim was immaculate. Mike killed four of Creasy's goons from his stomach within seconds, one shot per goon. Mike's heart thumped with rushing adrenaline.

"Mike, go get Katelyn!" Jim yelled.

As he rose, Mike cringed when he felt the old stab wound in his chest sizzle with pain. A bullet shot by Jim hammered a thug closing in on Mike. The thug collapsed as Mike sprang to his feet, darting down a narrow corridor. He followed the lingering shadows, steering away from the gun-fight, on the hunt for Creasy.

Flanagan skirted the boundaries of the shadows, steering away from the shooting match, as he discarded an empty clip from his Beretta, smelling the scent of sweet revenge that wafted through the catacombs. He had overheard Jim bark the orders to Mike and could feel the burning need to get to Creasy before Mike. He jacked his Beretta with his last clip, weaving through the ravine of the dead, meandering through the extensive graveyard in search for Creasy.

The echo of running footsteps lingered just yards ahead of him, almost mocking Flanagan. The tunnel veered to the right as Flanagan's light traced the curve in the skull-plastered wall. Flanagan swore he had lost five pounds from the moment he had plunged into the catacombs to now, but his suit weighed a ton, as it had absorbed buckets of his sweat. Peeling off his Armani coat and unleashing his throat from the clutches of his tie, Flanagan stripped down to his sweaty, white button-down and rolled the damp sleeves to his elbows, letting his hairy arms cool off. Leaving a trail of expensive clothing, Flanagan heard moans echoing from the dark.

"Shut up!" Creasy hissed in Katelyn's ear as Flanagan picked up the pace.

Mike's vision dwindled, becoming almost non-existent, unable to penetrate the thickening fog of blackness, forcing him to resort to his sense of touch. Feeling the walls of the catacombs, Mike shuttered as he ran his fingers over parts of ancient corpses. In high school, he had read a collection of stories by Edgar Allen Poe, one of them being *The Cask of Amontillado*. As Mike traversed through the braid of catacombs under Lynn, he could not help but relate to Fortunato, as he was also being led by a mad man.

A dark figure bolted from the shadows, darting across the slim corridor. Mike quickly raised his revolver. In the distance, he heard Katelyn's familiar voice moan. Mike swiftly crept down the murky corridor. His New Balance tennis shoes quietly propelled him forward as he sidled within three feet of the figure. "Alistair," Mike called out as dribbles of sweat streamed down his face, walking through the dank atmosphere. "I thought you wanted to settle this, huh? Mano-a-mano."

"I do, Mike," Creasy's voice echoed. "But, that doesn't mean I will let you kill me." The voice bounced in different directions around Mike. "You see, we all have our own destinies. This is all part of a greater plan."

The voice spun Mike in a dizzying tornado. His ears began ringing as he heard a muffled crunched under his foot. Smoke rose from the bottom of Mike's shoe and wafted toward his nose and mouth as he began coughing. Mike tried shielding his face from the potent gas, stumbling backwards. Soon, the corridor began rotating. Still coughing, Mike stumbled backwards into the moldy stone wall. Creasy bolted from a narrow crevice in between the masonry, as Mike collapsed on the cold ground; he aimed for Creasy's shoulder blades and squeezed the trigger. The bullets seemed to bounce off of Creasy as if he was made of steel. Then, Creasy mysteriously vanished into thin air. Mike fell back, incredibly weak, and slammed his head against the stone.

His vision had begun fading in and out of focus as his eyes lulled back into his head. He shivered as coldness showered him. His hands turned ghost white when a pretty finger wrapped around it. He felt the glowing smile of Katelyn shine down on him. He tried to smile back.

"You're okay, Mike," she said, stroking his face. "Everyone is safe." Katelyn whispered and kissed his forehead. Mike was unable to stay conscious. He plunged into a black hole that wiped his memory.

I still don't remember what happened next. Jim told me they found me unconscious with Katelyn kneeling by my side, clasping my frigid hand, and stroking my sweaty hair. He told me that I killed Flanagan in a blinding rage. I barely remember watching the smoke from the tip of my revolver evaporating into the walls of the catacombs. They called life support and evacuated me from the premises. I awoke from a three-day coma. The doctors said the toxin was carbon monoxide. Fortunately, it was not a concentrated dose, so the side effects were mild. The doctor added that carbon monoxide poisoning was very common, and said I would be fine. "We inhale it every day," The doctor said, and told me to call if my symptoms got worse. I thanked him and spent a few more days in bed. During my recovery, I talked to Jim about job opportunities at the police department and filled out an online application for rookie police officers.

As I look back at my younger self, I laugh, astonished by how green I was. Those days are far behind me. Katelyn and I are now married. The day we moved into our one-bedroom apartment in Boston, I treated everyone to dinner. Ruth's Chris Steakhouse had the perfect ambiance. The lighting was dim. Customers seated at tables and in booths talked quietly amongst their respective parties as they awaited their orders. We all stuffed ourselves. I ordered one of their signature filets, with their shoestring fries and fresh asparagus. Jim and Kathy decided on the Porterhouse for two and Katelyn ate the restaurant's petite filet. When I dug into my pocket to fish out the ten-carat diamond cluster engagement ring, Jim smiled and nodded approvingly. I had asked him earlier in the evening if he would allow me to become his son-in-law. "Why not?" he responded.

"You're already my adopted son. Keep things simple," he shrugged as he playfully clapped my shoulder. So, with Jim's approval, I was able to relax.

"Katelyn, will you marry me?" I asked, sliding the opened case between us on the table. "Yes," she replied.

The streets of Boston seemed so rough when I was a kid, but with good cops, Boston doesn't seem so rugged. Good cops are made. And with them around, Boston is a beautiful city.

END